The Sea Shack

by

Mark McNulty

The Sea Shack

ISBN-13: 978-1482794687
ISBN-10: 1482794683

Library of Congress Control Number: 2003099594

This book is printed on acid free paper

Printed in the United States of America

This book is dedicated to my grandfather,
Wilbur Fisher.

"If you give a man a fish,

he will eat for a day.

If you teach a man to fish,

he will eat for a lifetime."

Acknowledgements

Back in 2004, <u>The Sea Shack</u> marked my first adventure into the world of professional writing. Over the years, this story has changed my life in many wonderful ways. It is a story I remain tremendously proud of, and I feel my first priority is to thank the many special people who helped me along the way.

It begins with my parents, Robert and Beverly McNulty. I can never thank them enough for the unconditional support, love, and care they have always given me. Over the years I have learned how important it is to have a strong, loving family. I consider myself blessed to have grown up under their care and guidance. They, along with the support of my brother Bill, inspired me to do the things I truly wanted to do in life.

I would also like to thank all the teachers I had growing up. There are far too many to name, but they were the ones who convinced me I could be a writer and pushed me to improve. From kindergarten through college, they took the time to teach me the skills of an effective writer. Part of the reason I became a teacher myself is because they had such a powerful impact on my life. If I earn any praise for my writing, a big piece of the credit certainly belongs to them.

At my very first book signing in 2004, I signed a book for a young medical student named Carolyn. Little did I know we would begin dating a short time later and she would become my wife. I could not stop smiling when I met her that day, and she still brings a smile to my face today. She brings countless gifts into my world, from unconditional love to understanding and support, and I am lucky to be sharing my life with such an amazing woman.

I also need to thank the teachers and students at Saint Frances Cabrini School in San Jose, California. They were the first school to host me as a visiting author after they adopted <u>The Sea Shack</u> into their curriculum. I love to visit schools, talk with readers, and inspire new, young writers through my workshops. I understood that passion even better after that very first school visit, and I will always be grateful to them for that inspiring experience.

Finally, I owe a very special thank you to the many, many students I worked with as a teacher. They could be my strongest supporters and toughest critics at the same time. They shared their gifts of imagination, creativity, and enthusiasm with me every day. The children I worked with made teaching one of the most rewarding jobs around, and they will always inspire me to write good stories. I hope all of them know how special they are to me and that I will carry those gifts with me forever.

The Sea Shack

CHAPTER 1

If you ask me, the most challenging puzzles in the world are often the people who live around us. If you stop and think about it, you will know what I am talking about. Everyone knows at least one confusing person, a person you just can't understand. It may be someone in school, someone in your family, or just someone who lives on your street. Confusing people are those people you see and automatically begin asking questions about. Why does he do that? Why does she say things like that? Why doesn't he do this or that? What makes him tick?

Just like the puzzles you find in the store, these people puzzles can do two things: They can mesmerize you, or they can annoy you. They can draw you in and capture every bit of your attention. Somehow they make you want to be around them all the time, constantly discovering who they are and learning from them. Sometimes, though, these people puzzles are just too difficult. They frustrate you. They bewilder or perplex you, and you just want to walk away and leave them far behind.

In one crazy summer on Cape Cod, however, I learned something very important: The very best puzzles do both. Those puzzles that get your emotions completely fired up and occupy every tiny corner of your brain are the ones that will drive you absolutely crazy, but they are also the ones you can never let go of...

~~~~~~~~~~~~~~~~~~~~~~~~

When I was ten years old, finishing up my year in fourth grade, I thought I had the best life any kid could ever wish for. I probably should have worked harder in school back then, but that was not important to me when I was ten. To me, the only thing that was important was having fun. School meant nothing to me. The only thing it was any good for was getting to see my friends to talk about having fun! We would talk about video games, skateboarding, bikes, TV, movies, other kids, sports, family, toys—you name it. In fact, we would talk about almost anything as long it was something fun and had nothing to do with school.

Things were especially great for me because I had everything. I had always lived alone with my dad, and that was just fine by me. My dad loved me more than the world, and he did everything he could to make me happy. I had the best skateboard and the best bike of all my friends, nobody had more video games, and I was allowed to watch far more TV than any other ten-year-old in town! Whenever something new came out, something I knew I really needed, my dad would always get it for me as soon as he had the money. Even when I brought home bad grades, he would get upset for a while, but he was never too hard on me.

It wasn't like that for most of my friends. They didn't get as much or do as much because their mothers made too many rules for them. There was one line I would hear from my friends just about every day: "My mom won't let me." I used to feel so bad for them and wonder why their mothers were so mean. To me, my father loved me more than anything, and that was why he gave me so much and let me do whatever I wanted. I would look at my friend and wonder, If his mother loves him, why won't she let him do that? If she really loved him wouldn't she want him to have fun and be happy? In my fourth grade mind, it simply made no sense.

It was not just the things that my dad gave me that made him so great, but it was also what he did with me. Marshfield was a great town—at least I thought so. Sure, you could always find someone around town who had some problem with it, but I thought it was a great place to live. It was not a big, bustling city like Boston, but it wasn't like a farm town either. From its size to its people, Marshfield seemed to be right in the middle of the two. To begin with, we had a town center with a bunch of stores to shop in. It was a place where you could get almost anything from groceries to hardware. Furthermore, everywhere you went there was a pizza place or a Dunkin' Donuts to stop at, not to mention the Dairy Queen and McDonald's down the road. There were baseball fields, basketball courts, a skate park, and even trails through the woods where I could ride my bike. About the only thing missing was a movie theater, but there was one in a nearby town and it was easy to get to as long as you found someone to drive. Of course, my dad was great about that, too. If I couldn't get somewhere on my skateboard or bike, my dad would always take me in his truck. Sometimes on the weekends, he would also take me into Boston to see the city or to go to a Red Sox game. These trips were always fun. It was an incredible treat to walk around Boston and see all the buildings. So, naturally, back in fourth grade, I simply assumed I was the luckiest kid in school with the best dad in the world, and that my friends just weren't as lucky as I was. Yep, back then I thought I was all set, that I had it made, and that I was living the perfect childhood. My only fear was that things would somehow change, but I usually just assumed they would always stay the same.

Even though my father was so nice to me and gave me so many things, it never kept people from asking about my mother. There were other kids in my school who lived with only one parent, but their parents were divorced and at least those kids could say where the other parent was. They could tell stories about having breakfast with them, seeing them on weekends, or even taking vacations with them. I didn't have any stories about my mother.

I was just a baby when my mother died, and I don't even have one memory of her. All my dad and I had were a bunch of pictures of her and a few videos. One of the videos she made just for me when I was a baby. I watched it for the first time when I was about eight years old. In the video she is sitting in an old rocking chair and holding me tight. I am all wrapped up in a blue blanket, and she just keeps rocking me back and forth, looking at me the entire time. She tells me that I am more beautiful than she dreamed I would be and that she loves me. The video is not very long, but she says "I love you, Andy" more times than I can count, and she spends half the video crying. After I watched it, my dad told me I should keep it with me in a special place. I kept it, but it remained buried in the back of my closet from that day forward. I knew where it was, but I never thought about taking it out to watch again.

Don't get me wrong, it was nice having so many pictures and videos of my mother, but they weren't memories. Pictures and memories are two completely different things. My dad would look at the pictures and sometimes he would get choked up. If he knew I was watching, he'd do everything he could not to cry in front of me, but there were times that I saw him, or at least heard him in another room. He cried because he had all his memories of her. He dated her, married her, and had done many wonderful and exciting things with her, things that he missed doing. That's what made him cry. I could look at a picture or video screen for hours, but all I'd learn is what the person looked like. I never knew my mother and she never really knew me. I didn't have any memories and there was nothing for me to miss. All I had was one video and some pictures. I never cried.

The only problem I had with not having a mother was that it did make me angry sometimes. Not having a mother wasn't a big deal to me, but hearing the things some other kids would say was a big deal. As popular as I was with all my friends, there were some kids I did not get along with. Grades weren't my only problem in school; fighting was also a problem. The fights would always start the same way, too. There would be an argument, some name-calling, and then the other kid would say something about my mother and I'd swing my clenched fists at him to make him stop. Kids would say she hadn't really died, that she'd just left town to get away from me. Sometimes kids would say she was in jail, and some would say I didn't even have a mother, claiming I was a freak of nature or a space creature of some kind. They said these things to me all the time, and it always ended with me in the principal's office.

The fights weren't even the worst part: being in the office was. Mrs. Kensley, our principal, would ask me over and over again why I'd gotten into the fight. Then I would have to meet with Miss Peters, the school counselor, who would ask me questions about my mother. They both thought my fighting had to do with my mother and I could never explain to them that it wasn't about my mother: it was about the jerk who wouldn't leave me alone at recess. They would even try to convince my dad that the fighting was about my mother and that there was some kind of problem there. Lucky for me, my dad didn't listen. He'd talk to me about fighting but didn't ask all the questions Mrs. Kensley and Miss Peters would. My dad was never happy about my fights, but at least he understood me and listened to my reasons, instead of saying it had something to do with not having a mother around.

I think that was why living with my dad was so wonderful: I knew he understood me. Everyone had a bone to pick. My teacher, Mrs. Washburn, was always on my case about my grades. Mrs. Kensley and Miss Peters also pushed me to get better grades and never stopped asking about my mother. It was as if the three of them were all in a plot to drive me crazy by asking foolish, useless questions. Other adults who lived in our neighborhood would complain about me, saying I was too loud, or poorly behaved, or that I set a bad example. My friends were great, but even they'd give me a hard time or get upset with me once in a while. My dad truly was the only one who seemed to understand me.

He was the only one who listened to me and believed me when I told him things.

My dad was great. He listened to me. He did everything he could to make me happy. He always wanted the very best things for me. What more could I ask for? I didn't care if teachers, or principals, or neighbors, or anyone else had a problem with me. I knew my dad understood me and loved me, a3n0d I didn't need anything else. I was living the perfect life, with the perfect dad, in the perfect town. And then my worst fears started to come true: It all began to change.

CHAPTER 2

I remember that warm Friday in late May like it was yesterday. I can still see all the images in my mind, as if the day is being played back to me in slow motion, and everything that was said rings through my ears like it's on a broken CD that I can't stop. People usually remember the very best days of their lives forever and, unfortunately, they also remember the worst. This day was one of my very worst.

It started like any normal day. I got up at my usual time and had my breakfast, and then I took the bus to school and began my day. I was looking forward to school this day because my best friend, Kevin Gilman, was letting me borrow one of his video games. It wasn't one of the really popular games; it was just a driving game in which you race different cars through the city, but we loved playing it and he said I could borrow it. When I got to school though, he didn't have the game. We didn't get the chance to talk much before

Mrs. Washburn made us sit down and get ready for math, but I kept shooting him dirty looks the whole morning so he would know how annoyed I was. As usual, I didn't focus on math that morning. Instead, I focused on Kevin and how much he'd let me down by not bringing the game. I didn't even sit with him at lunch that day, and it wasn't until recess that I talked to him.

"Where is it? Why didn't you bring it?" I wanted an answer, I wanted to know why my so-called best friend didn't keep his promise.

"I'm sorry," he said. "I forgot it." Kevin never forgot anything. He was a human memory machine and I could tell he had just given me a very weak excuse. I kept asking him, following him, getting louder each time, badgering him, demanding to know why he hadn't brought the game.

"Look, Andy, my mother doesn't want me to let you borrow it unless I get one of yours. She said it is only fair if we trade." I couldn't believe what he was saying. What kind of friend was he?

"Trade?" I said with a gasp, as if I were in shock, "Trade? Are you kidding? My games are so much better than yours! You'd have to give me five of yours for it to be fair!"

"Shut up, Andy. Your games aren't that great. You probably wouldn't even give my game back. You'd probably just steal it." He was looking right into my eyes now and I knew he was angry with me. I felt that little voice inside me saying he was my best friend and I should calm down, but, as usual, I didn't listen to that voice. Besides, I was angry, too.

"You're such a little chicken, anyway, Kevin! You won't trade games with me because your stupid mother won't let you!" I began using the whiniest baby voice I knew and mocking him as loudly as I could: "Look at me! Kevin the baby! My mommy won't let me! My mommy won't let me!"

Just as he looked like he might begin to cry, he opened his mouth and violently fired back at me. "At least I have a mother! Your mother probably saw your face, realized what an idiot you are, and ran as far away as she could! I wouldn't want to be your mother either!"

All my senses were taken over by that old familiar feeling. My entire body became really tight, as if it was bunching up into a tiny ball, and then my hand suddenly flew right into his face. I jumped on Kevin and hit him as hard as I could. I called him every horrid name I could think of, trying to break him into two pieces before Mrs. Washburn and Mrs. Sanders, another fourth grade teacher, pulled us apart. We both sat in the office, staring each other down, and I couldn't digest that unsettling feeling that I was in for a long day.

I faced the usual string of questions from Mrs. Kensley and Miss Peters: Why did I start the fight? What was the big problem? Why couldn't I talk it out? And of course, the big ones came from Miss Peters. Why do I get so angry when kids say things about my mother? Why does it make me want to hit them? My mother, my mother, my mother—over and over again. For someone who didn't exist in my life, people sure loved asking about her.

My dad picked me up after school as usual and had another talk with Mrs. Kensley. As I got into the car, he was quieter than usual. I wondered if maybe he was really angry this time, angrier than normal. Was it something else? I didn't like seeing my father this quiet and I wondered what he was thinking about the whole ride home.

Back at the house, I didn't get to go out and play. I didn't feel like it, anyway. As angry as I was with Kevin, I did feel bad that I had gotten into a fight with him. He was my best friend, and now I wondered if we would ever be friends again. I usually didn't regret fights too much, but this was different. Whenever something bad happens with a friend, you hope and pray you can go back to the way things were but worry that they might never be the same. I had my usual talk with dad about fighting, and we spent more time talking about being friends with people. He gave me some advice on trying to be friends with Kevin again and on avoiding more fights. I felt a little better after our talk, but it was still a miserable day in the life of a fourth grader.

Just as I was going up to my room to watch some TV, my dad stopped me. "Andy, come back over here a minute. There's something else I need to talk to you about." I got a deep sinking feeling in my stomach, as if a giant black hole was opening up. Just from his tone, I knew my dad wasn't about to tell me anything good. I knew it wasn't going to be about a trip to Fenway Park or a day at the movies; it would be the type of thing I wasn't used to hearing him say.

"Listen, something has come up at work, and I need to go away for a while. It won't be a long time, just a couple months during the summer. I'd really like to stay here, believe me, but this is a big opportunity for me and it is really important that I go. Do you understand?"

I nodded slowly, thinking about what he had said and not feeling quite so bad now. "Yeah, Dad. I understand. It will be fun. I like taking trips with you anyway, and this will just be like a big vacation. Where are we going anyway? When do we leave? Is anyone else going that you know?" I actually began to get excited about a summer trip. My mind began to race, thinking

16

of all the incredible places I had heard about in school, wondering if we were going to a place like Hawaii, Florida, or California. Then, with a few short words from my father, it all came to a screeching halt.

"Andy, I can't take you," he said quietly.

I stared into his eyes in total shock, trying to hold back the pools of sadness that instantly began to build in my eyes. I didn't want to cry in front of my father, but I couldn't believe he had said that to me.

"I have to go to Texas on a business trip. I'm sorry, Andy, but I can't take you. I wish I could: honest I do. I wish I could stay here. I wish I could be with you, but I can't. This job is too important. I *have* to go, but I will be back before the summer is over, I promise."

I felt like I couldn't breathe, as if all the air and life had been sucked out of me. This was my dad, the best dad in the entire world, telling me he wasn't going to spend the summer with me, telling me he had to leave me. Somehow, I reached inside my throat and pulled out a few soft words, "Where am I going to go?"

He took a deep breath and softly grabbed my shoulders. He looked down as if he were searching for the words on the floor, and then he looked into my eyes again. "I talked to your grandfather. He said he would love to have you stay with him this summer. He thinks it would be great, and I think you'll like it, too. I know—"

Before he could finish I cut off his words, taking a tone that was half disbelief and half anger now. "Grampy? I'm going to live with *Grampy*? He hardly even knows me!"

"Andy, listen to me. This is the best that we can do. It will all be fine, you'll see. The two of you can—"

I cut him off again, throwing his hands off my shoulders. "It *won't* be fine! It will be the worst summer ever! Why are you doing this to me? Why are you leaving me? Don't you love me? Aren't *I* important enough to you?"

"Of course I love you, Andy, that's why I—"

"NO!" I was determined to keep him from talking. "If you loved me you would stay! You'd stay if you loved me! I'm going to hate living at Grampy's and I hate you for making me go!" I turned my back to him and sprinted up to my room as the tears came streaking down my cheeks. I slammed the door behind me and dove into my bed. He knocked to come in but I angrily told him to stay away from me. I sat in my room crying for hours, trying not to let my dad hear me. I wanted him to know how angry I was at him, but I didn't want him to know how hurt I was. I cried until I fell asleep, never even thinking about dinner. I was *that* upset, angry to the point where I completely overlooked the thought of food. Even after I fell asleep, I woke up many times. I kept thinking about how my summer was already ruined and it wasn't even June yet. I kept trying to understand why my father would do this to me. Worst of all, I couldn't help but imagine how agonizing and boring the summer with my grandfather would be.

A day that had begun with so much excitement over a video game had ended as the very worst day in my entire life. I had possibly lost my best friend in a fight, and I suddenly found myself hating my father. He was going away without me, ruining my entire summer. I swore that night that I would never forgive him for it.

CHAPTER 3

Of all the people I knew, my grandfather was the last person I would ever want to spend a summer with. I knew who he was, but that was about all I could say about him. I couldn't begin to understand why my father would make me live with someone like *him*. I had cousins and aunts and uncles I could stay with. Why didn't my father have me go and stay with them instead?

My earliest memories of my grandfather were from when I was a small toddler. He would come and visit the house from time to time, even stay overnight once in a while. Mostly, he would spend his time talking with my dad or helping him around the home, but he would always make sure to spend some time with me, too. We would play in the yard if it was a nice day, and if it wasn't a day to be outside he'd tell me jokes or watch a movie with me. Those movies quickly got boring, though, because they were usually history movies on TV, the ones with some old guy talking and all the pictures in black and white. They just weren't the movies I wanted to see as I grew older. In a way, they were just like the man himself—old, boring, and gray.

It didn't matter that much, anyway, because as I grew older I saw my grandfather less often. I figured he had probably come around a lot when my mother was alive, but after she died he didn't have any reason to come anymore. There had been fewer visits each year and eventually they stopped completely. Sure, he got along with my father, but I think his biggest reason for visiting was to see his daughter. After she passed away, I guess it simply became too much trouble to come and say hello. So, why would he want me to come and stay with him now? I hadn't seen him at all in three or four years, and I found it very hard to believe that he would want me living with him. I almost became angry that he had stopped coming to our house but still expected me to go to his house for the whole summer. I kept thinking about how unfair things could be. I thought about the fight I'd had with Kevin, how his mother had said it was only fair if we traded games. To me, it wasn't fair that I had to stay with a grandfather who never came to see me.

Even though my grandfather didn't visit us anymore, I knew some things about him. He lived by himself in a town called Truro on Cape Cod. I had seen his house in pictures, and it was really small. It was right on the beach and I assumed that made him happy. Marshfield had beaches, but I never went. I didn't see any point in going to the beach. It just didn't seem like any fun to me. Whenever my father talked with the family members, he would ask how the Captain, my grandfather, was doing or what he had been up to lately. My uncles called him "The Captain," probably because he used to love taking people out on his boat for fishing trips. I heard many stories about these fishing trips and the things that happened on them. Sometimes they were funny stories, and sometimes they were stories that sounded pretty scary. It was not unusual at all for my uncle to be having dinner with us and to start talking about what "The Captain" had been doing lately. It was almost always something boring, though. He didn't even have a boat any longer, and I never heard about him making those great fishing trips any more. To me, he was just a boring old man who lived all by himself.

Of course, I never called him "Captain," — probably because I had never gone fishing with him or shared any of these adventures with him. I just called him "Grampy." Whenever I talked about him or asked about him, it was always "Grampy" I asked about. I would only ask about him if my father was already talking about him, though. Most of the time, he never crossed my mind. It is hard to think about things, never mind talk about things, that you never see.

Some kids have four loving grandparents. Their grandparents shower them with wonderful gifts or slip them money when their parents aren't watching. Some kids have grandparents who take them on trips or go to their soccer games to cheer them on. I knew some kids in school who were always spoiled rotten by their grandparents. I didn't have this. I only had one grandparent, and he was an old man I never saw. Much like my mother, he was someone who really meant nothing to me, a person who was not important in my life. He kept to himself, never came to visit, and didn't even call to talk to me on the phone. As best I could tell, Grampy was just a lonely, sad old man who lived by the sea and did absolutely nothing with his life.

CHAPTER 4

The rest of the school year seemed to drag by like a massive weight being pulled by a lazy mule. Everything had changed that Friday afternoon. My grades got even worse, I got into more fights, and I didn't enjoy being around my dad any longer. I did begin talking to Kevin again, but we weren't friends like we had been before. Some of my other friends didn't hang around me as much either, saying they didn't like the way I had treated Kevin. It felt as if Kevin and I had a contest to see who would keep more friends, and he was winning. Usually having lots of friends was the most important thing to me, but I had a hard time thinking about that now. I was still angry that my summer had been ruined. I was still angry with my father. For the last four weeks of the school year, I tried to talk to him as little as possible, and I made sure we didn't have any fun together those days.

I knew work was important to my father, but it had never come between us before. I didn't know what he did exactly, but I knew he worked in a very tall building in Boston. He used to show me his building when we took trips into the city. It was huge, so I knew his job must be a really important one if he got to work in a building like that! The company he worked for was a big bank, but he didn't work at the counter handing out money like other people in banks. He had his own office and all he ever worked on was computer stuff. He had convinced his boss to let him do some work at home, so he could pick me up at school each day, but even when he was doing work at home, it was always on the computer. It must have been a hard job because he worked very late at night after I went to bed. He made sure he spent time with me first, though, and then did his work at night. That was why I was so upset now. I just couldn't understand it. I mean, he got out of work early to pick me up at school and he saved his work for night so he could spend time with me. So why couldn't he stay home with me now? Why was he leaving me? He had changed things to be with me before, so why couldn't he change them again? I sat in bed wide awake almost every night that June, thinking to myself and even crying sometimes, wondering why my father was betraying me like this.

It was bad enough having all those questions in my head, feeling angry inside, resenting my father for what he was doing; but I foolishly made it even worse by letting people at school find out. I had told my friends where I was going for the summer, and of course they told everyone else. Now they didn't just have my mother to make jokes about: they also got to say things about my dad. Toby Sullivan, who was the biggest bully in the fourth grade, came to me at recess one day and really gave it to me.

"Hey, Andy!" He used one of those mocking tones only kids can do well. "What's the matter? Your father is running away now, too! First your mother gets away from you—now your dad!" He began to lead his friends in laughing at me. As you may have guessed, that turned into a fight and another visit to the office.

Another kid, Jeff Delpart, who wasn't really a bully but a kid who never stopped talking, took a different approach. "Hey, Andy!" Again there was that whiny, mocking tone of voice: "I heard you're not even going to your grandfather's house. I heard you're really being sent to boot camp! Nobody could stand being around you so they had to send you away!"

All the kids laughed, and I reacted the same way I usually did when I was teased. Before I knew what was happening, I was sitting in the office again for getting into another fight. It was probably the worst time of my entire life because everything was falling apart. My friends, my school work, and my relationship with Dad all seemed to be breaking into tiny crumbs before my very eyes. Worst of all, I could do nothing to stop it and I blamed my father for the entire thing.

Finally, fourth grade ended, and the day came when I was supposed to go to my grandfather's house. I tried everything I could to stay home. I refused to get out of bed, lying there like a rock until my father finally dragged me out. Next, I decided that if I didn't get dressed, I couldn't leave the house and I'd *have* to stay home. This trick failed, too. My father had all my stuff packed in the truck already except for the clothes I was wearing to Grampy's, which were hanging up on my door. When he saw me sitting frozen in my chair, not dressed, he let out a big sigh. I knew he was getting frustrated with me.

"I'll carry you into the truck if I have to, Andy, and I don't think you want your grandfather meeting you in those PJs." He had a good point, but I would never have admitted that. I waited until he'd left my room and then slowly got dressed. The next plan was to skip breakfast, but I was again met with failure.

My father simply said out loud, as he busily packed the truck, "All animals need to eat and that includes you, Andy. Any animal will eat when he gets hungry enough, and you will too. Skip breakfast if you want; I know you'll be eating soon." I was pretty hungry, so I waited until he wasn't looking and had my bowl of cereal. I was getting more upset every minute, realizing that every plan I came up with failed almost as soon as I thought of it.

On the ride to Truro, I made sure not to smile at all. My father kept working to make me feel better and I was doing my best impression of a stone wall. I would not crack, I would not giggle, and I would not smile. Most of all, I would not cry. He kept saying the same things he had been saying for weeks: This was for the best, he had no choice, he couldn't bring me, he would if he could, he was going to miss me, he'd try to call me, and it would be better than I thought. They were all lies. I knew what the real truth was: He didn't want to be around me and he was leaving me, plain and simple. He had turned on me. Finally, I got tired of him telling me these same things over and over and I spat out the words that I knew hurt him most: "I hate you."

"Don't say that, Andy. You don't hate me. You may not like what we need to do, but you—"

"No! I *do* hate you! You're making me do this, so I hate you!" I knew it hurt him to hear me say that, but it hurt me to see him leave. At school I had gotten into fights with hands, but I could never do that with my father. This was my way of fighting back against him.

After a long, miserable ride, we finally pulled up to a tiny white house by a sand dune. I didn't think it was even big enough to be a house; it was more like a

32

cottage, or maybe even a shack. The driveway was just an area of crushed clamshells and the mailbox looked like an old lobster trap, only smaller. There was no yard—at least not like the kind I was used to. Around the driveway there was lots of sand and fields of tall green grass beyond that. I walked into it, but it was sharp and prickly and bit into my legs, so I scampered out. A small path went all around the house, and to one side was a garden. It was a good-sized garden, almost the same size as the shack, and a tall flagpole stood right in the middle of it. The front door did not face the street; instead, it faced the ocean. A long path led from the front door, through an even larger field of the biting grass, and down to the water. The only other thing I could see aside from the shack was a shabby, beat-up picnic table and a rusty grill near the front door. As I looked at the tiny shack by the sea, I thought. *This can't be where I am going to live.* My impression was that if you looked up "boring" in the dictionary, right next to the word you would see a picture of this shack.

As I was staring at this scene in a state of shock, an old man slowly walked around the corner. It was closer to a lumber or a waddle than a walk, and I knew right away it was my grandfather. You see all those movies where kids run to their grandparents and throw their arms around them for a giant hug, grandfather's spinning the children around, calling them cute nicknames like "Tiger" or "Champ," and then handing them some special prize with a wink of the eye. Well, in my case, that was not what happened. I would not be giving any hugs, and I didn't expect any prizes. I just gave both men angry stares, as if my eyes could make them break down and cancel the whole plan.

My father unloaded my stuff from the truck and brought it inside while my grandfather came over to me, asking short questions between long pauses. "Hello there, Andy. Remember me? You ready for a great summer?" He had such a unique voice. It was smooth, but also scratchy. It wasn't soft, but it also wasn't loud. It had sort of a warmth to it. It was not the weak little voice many old men have, the ones you can hardly hear, but it was definitely the voice of an older person. It was strong and clear but gave you the impression it was a voice that had spoken to many people and traveled to many places over time. I didn't say anything back to him: I only stared.

"Do you like the beach?" he asked.

Again, my only answer was a stare.

"Well, don't talk if you don't want to; it will just be a quiet summer, I guess."

With that, I grew tired of staring at him and began staring at the ground, kicking at the crushed clamshells and leaning against the truck. I looked at those clamshells, and I sympathized with them. They were once happy clams living in the ocean, living the perfect life, before someone took them from their home and smashed them into tiny ivory and gray fragments. I, too, was happy in my home and living the perfect life—right before my father smashed it all.

Just then, my father came back over to me. He went down on one knee and held onto my shoulders again. "Andy," he said softly, "I need to get going now to catch my flight to Dallas. All your stuff is inside and ready to be unpacked. Hey, look at me." He was speaking softly, and I knew he was hurting, but I wouldn't give him the satisfaction of seeing my face. There was no way I'd look up.

"Andy, things will be fine. Trust me on this, okay? I love you and—"

"No!" My head flipped up like it was on a spring and I threw his hands off me like they were deadly spiders. Those three words had set me off. "You don't love me! If you loved me you'd stay! Don't you get it! Fathers who love their kids don't leave them! I hate you!"

I wanted to be sure those were the last words I said to him and I ran from the truck as fast as I could. I wanted to run to my room, my own room, in my own house, in my own town where everything had once seemed perfect, but I couldn't. All those things were over an hour away from me. I wanted a safe place that was all my own but I had nothing here. I just ran down the sandy path, past all the biting grass, all the way down to the beach until I stumbled on a piece of wood and crashed into the sand. I put my head between my knees and began to cry uncontrollably. I looked back once and could see my father and grandfather talking behind me, but neither one came over to me for a long time. I felt the tears running down my face and didn't care who saw me. I didn't really care about anything at that moment: I just wanted the nightmare summer to end.

I must have been on that beach for hours, crying until my eyes seemed to dry up on me. At just about the same moment, I heard soft footsteps in the sand behind me. It was my grandfather. I just sat there, waiting for what he was going to say. It was getting dark and I was sure he was going to try to make me feel better. I was ready for him to sit down next to me, put an arm around me, and do his very best to comfort me. I was ready for him to say how happy he was to have me, how much my father loved me, and how much fun we were going to have together. Instead, he said only one thing: "If you're gonna sleep on the beach, keep one eye open for the wolves." And then he walked away, back to his tiny shack on the beach.

My first reaction was to turn my head upright and say a loud, confused "huh?" to myself. He had completely surprised me. My second reaction was a nervous one. Wolves? What wolves? I began looking around me, looking into the biting grass as darkness slowly crept up and covered my eyes. I saw a yellow flash in the grass. A lightning bug? Or the hungry eyes of a wolf? I didn't know if he was serious or not, but I didn't want to take the chance. I quickly got to my feet and scampered after him. When I got inside, dinner was waiting for me: pork chops and baked beans. All that crying had made me hungry so I sat down and quietly ate my food, looking at my grandfather from time to time out of the corner of my eye. I'd always believed I could outsmart anyone around me, but he had won this battle. He must have wanted me to come in, sit down, and eat dinner, and he got his way. Other adults had spent hours, days, even weeks trying to make me do what they wanted me to do, but I was a world champion at holding my ground and never giving in. My grandfather had made me do exactly what he wanted with one simple sentence. Part of me felt embarrassed that I had been defeated by a foolish old man, yet, secretly, I was a little impressed by his win. My education with Grampy had begun.

CHAPTER 5

After dinner that night, Grampy showed me around the house. There was only one floor in the shack, not even a basement. The entire living area was only four rooms, five if you counted the tiny bathroom. The front door, facing the ocean, opened up into a room that was both a dining area and living room. A small, shabby table with two rickety chairs stood by the window and an old, dusty sofa lined one whole wall. The sofa was soft from years of use and it was a pale shade of yellow I had never seen before. Next to the sofa was a small wooden stand holding an old black and white TV on top and, under that, a tiny radio on a shelf. I had never seen a TV with an antenna on it before, having grown up with cable my whole life. I spent about a minute studying that antenna, sticking up from the TV at a crazy angle, and wondered how he could be happy with something so ancient.

Next to that main room was a small kitchen with only the basic needs: a slightly rusted white stove, a metal sink, a fridge that was a nasty lime green color, and a rack near the ceiling that held an assortment of battered pots and pans. About the only modern piece of cooking equipment in this kitchen was a tiny black microwave stored in the corner. Without any rust, scratches, or obvious stains, it stuck out like a sore thumb.

Finally, in the back, there were two bedrooms: his with a large bed in it, taking up most of the room, the other, an even smaller room with a twin bed in it that would be mine for the summer. My stuff was already in there and my grandfather told me I could set the room up any way I wanted. "This is your room for the summer, Andy. Keep it clean and make yourself at home."

Calling this a house was definitely a stretch for me. How could you call it a house when it was barely big enough for two people? It really seemed much more like a shack than a house. As my eyes scanned my temporary home, the same thought kept lingering in my head, like a fog refusing to leave the ground: How was I going to survive living here?

The tour did not end with the inside of the house. Grampy also pointed out the picnic table by the front door, noting that it was nicer to eat out there in the summer than to sit inside. He warned me to keep things weighed down so the wind wouldn't steal them, and to keep an eye on my food so the gulls wouldn't steal it. "They are like bandits," he said. "The minute you stop watching, they'll swoop down and snatch your meal right off the plate." I couldn't imagine them being *that* bad, but as I looked at one of the shifty-eyed gulls out for an evening stroll, I decided my grandfather probably knew what he was talking about.

After my brief tour of his tiny home and the area around it, my grandfather sat on the sofa to watch TV. My mixed-up insides began to settle down some, and I got the crazy idea that maybe I should try talking to my grandfather. Mr. Conroy, my third grade teacher, had once said that if you can't change something, you

41

should try to make the best of it. Well, this was beginning to look like a situation I couldn't change. I knew that conversation wasn't one of my strengths, but I wanted to give it a try.

"Grampy?" I said softly. "Are there really wolves out there?"

He chuckled a bit before peering over at me. "Naw, you won't find any wolves out there. But, on some dark nights, the winds off the ocean can get pretty biting and make a noise just like the howl of a wolf. It is quite a sound." A little smile flashed on his face before he admitted to his trick. "It was enough to get you inside, though, huh?"

I let that digest for a few minutes before making up my mind whether or not to continue to try to be friendly. I was actually growing a little tired of being angry the entire time and also knew it had not gotten me anywhere. Question number one had gone fairly well, so I boldly decided to try another one. "What are you watching, Grampy?" Anger and resentment were still smoldering in me, so it was hard to muster a very friendly voice. While I am not very good at conversation, however, I am even worse at being silent.

He didn't even look at me, but simply said, "The news."

The news? We were going to watch the news? Wasn't there something better than the useless old news on TV? The news was boring! I didn't want to watch the news! Suddenly, as if he was able to read my mind, he slowly turned to look at me, a strange smile on his face. "Well, I suppose you think you can find a better program, huh? Why not give it a try."

I leaned forward and reached for the TV eagerly. This was more like it; he was already letting me decide what to watch on the TV. His set did not have a remote, so I needed to use the buttons on the set itself. We were watching the news on channel four now, so I moved up to five. More news. I hit the channel button again, and found yet another news program on channel six. Channel seven was even more news. I knew there must be a movie on somewhere, but when I hit the channel button again it went back to four. I must have gone through channels four, five, six, and seven about ten times, increasing the flipping speed each time, before I sat back completely exasperated. I heard my grandfather let that soft chuckle out again, the one I was beginning to understand as a sign he had outfoxed me.

"You only have four channels on your TV?" I asked him with a shade of shock in my voice, praying desperately that he'd tell me there were more.

"Yep, four seems to be plenty for me. What do you do? Watch cable all day? The only TV you need is right here." My grandfather was getting a good laugh from this, but I wasn't amused at all. It was just one more frustrating spoke in this wheel of boredom. I loved TV! I watched it every day, but having no cable was going to make my passion a struggle. I tried my best to watch the news but only made it about two minutes before I gave up and went into my room.

As I unpacked my things, I dwelt on what was becoming the obvious: This summer was getting worse by the minute. I was still furious with my father for leaving me, and even when I tried to find something good in this crummy old shack, it quickly turned out bad. I got my things put away and went to bed for the night, trying to fall asleep in the cable-less, run-down, cramped, crowded, boring old man's sea shack.

Before I knew it, I was awake—and I wasn't happy about it! It had taken me forever to fall asleep, and it seemed like my eyes had just closed when I was startled by a loud clanging noise over my head. CLANG! CLANG! CLANG! I jumped from my bed in shock. It kept ringing in my ears like a rapid-fire noise machine, and it only got louder when I covered my head with my pillow. CLANG! CLANG! CLANG! I finally opened my eyes, looked up, and saw my grandfather standing over me, banging a metal pan with a spoon.

"Out of bed, sleepy head! Rise and shine!" He was full of energy and I wondered just how late I had slept in. I looked at the old clock hanging on the wall and couldn't believe my eyes: 6:15 A.M.

"What are you doing, Grampy?" My voice was nothing but a low, slow, moany, groany whine. "It's too early. I'm still sleeping."

"Not in this house you're not! Let's go, out of bed!"

I did not budge an inch. I stayed in bed, placed my head firmly on the pillow, and let him bang away at his metal pan. It was a showdown, a match between the old man and me. I had no idea why he wanted me out of bed so early, but I was not going to give in. He clanged away at that pan for a few more minutes. Then he let out a disgusted grunt. He gave me a long, hard look of disapproval before he finally gave up and left the room. I had won. He tried his best to get his way, but he lost. I wanted to sleep some more, but a huge smile crept across my face. I couldn't help but smile. This was a big moment for me, a move in the right direction. If I wanted to enjoy this summer, I had to make sure Grampy left me alone and let me do things my way. He needed to learn that I was my own boss. I felt like my face was going to split down the middle, I was smiling so hard. Then I heard footsteps coming into the room.

SPLASH! Before I'd even had the chance to think about those footsteps, before I could even predict what was about to happen, before I was able to devise any sort of new plan, I was on my feet and out of bed, shivering with cold. The old man stood there, chuckling at me with his empty bucket. I thought I had won, but I had just lost *badly*. In my glorious, fleeting, moment of victory, he had filled a bucket with ice water and returned to pour every drop of it over my resting body. Not only was I out of bed, but I was WIDE awake now. I was too cold to speak, nearly too cold even to think. He just looked me over, chuckling and shaking his head. Finally, he handed me a towel.

"Dry off and come to breakfast."

As soon as I was dried off I went out for breakfast, just as he had told me. I now had a new plan. I needed to face off with him and get him to leave me alone. I was going to get right in his face and tell him exactly what was on my mind. That plan, however, was shaken quite a bit when I saw the stack of pancakes on the table. I don't know if it was luck or if my father had told him, but pancakes were a fatal weakness of mine. Just as Superman broke down near kryptonite, I was sure to break down around pancakes. Seeing that stack of golden brown, piping hot flapjacks stole all the words right out of my mouth—only for a moment, but long enough for him to steal my thunder.

"Listen to me and listen to me good, Andy. You are in *my* house now, and you will live by *my* rules. I don't care what you do at home or what your father says at home. I am the boss now, and what I say around here is the law."

He wasn't yelling, but his voice was firm and strong, and he was looking directly at me. His eyes were locked steadily on my face, and I cowered down slightly as he spoke to me. "I don't care when you go to bed, but you will be up by 6:30 every morning. You will help out around here and you *will* do work. If you think you are going to sleep the summer away and make nothing of your time, you are dead wrong. I'm happy to have

48

you here, but you're going to live by my rules: nobody else's. Are we understood?"

I didn't want to say anything. I couldn't figure him out at all. I couldn't figure out what he wanted me to say or what he wanted me to do. I felt that if I said anything, it would be the wrong thing. For some reason, though, I couldn't stay silent. I'd never had a problem staying silent with my father, or teachers, or anyone else I'd ever met. It had always worked for me, too, but I had the feeling it wouldn't work with my grandfather. There was something about Grampy, something that made me want to answer him, even if it meant giving the wrong answer. I softly spoke up, "Yes, understood...but...can't I at least sleep later? This is too early for me." I gave him the most innocent, sorry, sad look I had, the really pitiful one I used only in emergencies when I absolutely, positively *needed* to get something my way.

He looked at my face, put his fork down while he chewed his pancakes, and then said something I have never forgotten to this very day: "You'll have plenty of time to sleep when you're gone.

CHAPTER 6

Over the next few days, I learned more and more about my grandfather. For the most part, he remained a mystery, but I was starting to figure him out. The most obvious thing about him was that he followed the same routine every day. It was as if he was a human clock, following an exact schedule Monday through Sunday. At almost any time, day or night, I would know where he was because his routine was so predictable.

I never knew exactly what time he woke up because he was always the first one up. I quickly realized I was *not* going to sleep in. I grew tired of the metal clangs of cookware over my head, and I never wanted an icy sunrise shower again, so I made sure I got out of bed when he told me to, no matter how painful it was.

By six o'clock every morning, breakfast was cooking and we were eating within a half hour. As much as I hated being in that shack and as horrible as waking up at the crack of dawn was, I must admit I soon looked forward to breakfast. Some mornings it would be golden pancakes and sometimes it would be French toast. Other times he would make waffles. One of my favorites was something he called a bull's eye. A bull's eye was nothing more than a piece of toast with a hole in the middle, filled with a cooked egg, usually sunny-side-up—A simple breakfast that anyone could make, but one I'd only started eating after learning about it from Grampy. Other mornings he would prepare bacon and eggs, hashed browns, sliced ham, omelets, or even fish (which was my least favorite for breakfast). Both of us would enjoy orange juice each morning with breakfast, a nice large glassful, not the tiny ones they give you in restaurants.

Once breakfast was done, he would walk outside to the garden. He'd inspect the garden for about five minutes and then come back into the house, go into his closet, and take out a perfectly folded American flag. He would take the flag outside to the pole and carefully raise it up high so it could fly over his tiny sea shack. This was an interesting ritual to watch: he never hurried to get it done. Even one morning when it was rather cold out, he did not hurry to get back inside but took the same care he had every other morning. It was a morning ritual that he performed faithfully, in any weather except heavy rain, and I came to enjoy watching him.

Only after he'd inspected the garden and raised the flag did he have his morning coffee—always two cups, never one cup and never three cups, always two. Coffee was something else he enjoyed slowly, sitting at the rickety, wobbly table and looking out over the ocean. When he drank his coffee at that tiny table, he wore the most unusual look on his face. It was a calm, quiet face, but it made me wonder what he was thinking about. He had the expression of a man who had a million ideas racing through his mind but was at total peace at the same time. Later in life, he would tell me that he had done some of his best thinking while sitting at that table with his coffee, simply watching the ocean rumbling away outside.

He would spend the rest of the morning doing any number of jobs around the house. It amazed me how busy he kept himself. With such a small house and so few neighbors, you would think he'd have nothing to do, but Grampy rarely sat still. He was constantly fixing something, building something, cooking something, or changing something to make it better. At 11:00 A.M. sharp, he would stop his work and sit on a chair by the door to read. This was another certainty in Grampy's day. He would spend that full hour each day, between eleven and noon, reading a book. Exactly at noontime, he would make lunch for us. We'd eat it outside at the picnic table, and then he'd go back to reading. He made sure lunch always lasted right up to 12:45, and then he would begin reading again, stopping at 2:00 to finish his work for the day.

There was another piece of his routine that always puzzled me. At four o'clock each afternoon, he would take the same glass out of the cabinet, fill it with a red wine, and slowly drink it while watching a judge on TV. It was one of those shows where people agree to have their case on TV and you watch them argue over it. There were two different ones and he would watch either one on any given day. Eventually, I began to enjoy the shows myself. It wasn't the show that puzzled me, however: it was the wine. I had seen adults drink wine from nice glasses with dinner; I had seen adults drink wine at parties. But I had never seen this before: He just took a normal glass, poured wine into it, and drank it while watching his show. He never had any more than one glass, and he never missed a day. In fact, he once came in from working outside and realized it was past four o'clock. For the rest of the day, it seemed to throw everything out of order for him, even though he only missed the time by about ten minutes. It was always this part of his routine that puzzled me the most because there did not seem to be any real reason behind it.

Dinnertime was at six o'clock sharp. No matter what day it was, dinner was at six. Of course, once in a while it would be a little later for one reason or another, but as long as Grampy was in control, he made sure we ate at six. Over the entire summer, I think there were only a handful of nights when dinner wasn't ready on time. Anything in the world could be going on, but I always knew dinner would be at six.

Just as lunch was over at 12:45 each day, dinner was over by 6:45 each night. That was when he would wash his hands, go outside, and take the flag down for the night. He would carefully lower it and then fold it up to bring it inside. It impressed me, the way he folded the flag. He was able to fold that flag in a way that it made a perfect triangle. Every time he lowered it, he folded it perfectly on his first try. I couldn't even fold my paper the right way during math, but he was able to fold this flag perfectly, without fail. He treated the flag like it was made of gold and everything he did with it was done with great care, almost like a surgeon who doesn't want to make a single error.

Once the flag was put away, it would be time for the news. Every station (all four) had a news program on at six, but Grampy almost never watched those programs. Instead, he watched one that was on at seven. It was the only one on at that time so there wasn't much of a choice. I never knew if he watched this one because it was his favorite, or because it was the only one that fit into his rigid routine.

When the news ended at eight, he would clean the dishes in the sink. He was a master at cleaning anything. Whether it was dishes in the sink or the old truck outside, he could get anything to sparkle. I have never met anyone who got dishes any cleaner than my grandfather did, and I never met anyone who could clean them faster either. In nearly no time at all, the dishes would be done and he would be ready to watch a little TV before going to bed at 9:30 each night. He went to bed at 9:30, but he did not go to sleep then. He would turn on the radio by his bed and listen to talk radio for exactly one hour, and then turn it off and go to sleep. Once in a while, if it was an especially good topic, he would stay up until eleven—but never a minute later.

Without this routine, I wonder how well he would have been able to function. It seemed like he had to get every step done at the exact time or the entire day would collapse. Just like the sun rises every day at a specific time, I knew that Grampy would complete certain tasks every day at a specific time: breakfast by 6:30, reading at eleven, lunch at noon, reading until two, wine at four, dinner at six, news at seven. It was a cycle that repeated itself day after day and never faltered. As soon as I'd learned the pattern of his routine, I hit upon an idea. I had the idea that if I could change his routine, or at least mess it up somehow, he would be forced to break down and let me have my way. I was sure he would crumble if the daily routine was shaken, and I was entirely confident that I could do just that. What I did not realize, however, was that he had already figured this out. The old man didn't let on, but he was anticipating my every move. I was determined to fight this daily schedule of his. I was determined to break it apart, but he was even more determined than I was, determined to make me part of it. It was the routine he lived by and one he believed in. One way or another, it was a routine he was certain I would learn.

CHAPTER 7

I had only been living with Grampy for three days before things really began to come crashing down on me. I thought life had been hard on me already and I was not prepared for it to get even worse, but compared to what was coming, those first three days were the easy ones. While I *did* have to get up early, I did *not* have to do much else. I watched whatever was on TV, took a few walks down by the beach, listened to a few Red Sox games on the radio, and basically tried to survive my life in this tiny black hole. Through it all, I continued to blame my father for the mess I was in. Whenever my anger towards him began to simmer down, I would remember something that would help it boil up again. It was as if I was keeping myself angry on purpose. For whatever reason, I did not want to let the anger go. I felt like that would make it too easy on my dad. Even when he called on my second night there, I refused to talk to him on the phone. My grandfather gave me a stern look of disappointment but did not make me take the phone. Either he understood how I felt or he just didn't want to get me angry again. Either way, he didn't force me to take the phone. In fact, there were very few things he did force me to do those first three days. I still hated being stuck there, but I was glad to have the freedom he had given me. All good things must come to an end, however, and that precious freedom came to a thundering end on my fourth day with Grampy.

I had finished my breakfast and he had already hung the flag up for the day. I got up from my seat and decided to walk down near the beach. There was still nothing I really enjoyed about the beach, but going down there was something to do. It was easy enough and it helped me pass some time. Plus, on some mornings, I would actually see or hear something interesting on the beach, such as a passing ship or a scurrying crab. So, with the hope of seeing something new on my mind, I got up from my seat, pushed in my chair, took my dishes to the sink, and began to make my way out the door.

"Where are you going?" my grandfather asked.

"I'm going down to the beach. Why?"

"Just don't go too far. Be back here in ten minutes so we can start working on the house today. Okay?" He said this as if we had planned to work together, as if we had arranged to be partners on a project. It was all news to me.

"*We?* What do you mean *we?* I didn't agree to do anything."

"I told you the other day, Andy. I told you that you aren't just going to sit around all summer, that you'd have to help out and do some work. That work starts today." He was not angry or upset at all, just very calm and firm in telling me what the plan was.

"What do I have to do?" I was hoping it might be an easy job. I was really trying not to get too upset before hearing what, exactly, he had in mind.

"You're going to help me paint the house. It looks like a mess and needs a new coat. We start today, in ten minutes."

I took a few short, panicky gasps, thinking of how much I was going to despise painting but trying to keep myself under control. "I'll do something but I'm not painting the house. It's *your* house; *you* paint it!"

Keeping that same firm, calm tone, he looked up at me and offered one of his typically direct responses, "As long as you're living here, it's your house too. We're both painting it, so be back here in ten minutes."

I twisted my head from side to side and shuffled my feet in a nervous little dance, and a stream of odd noises came from my mouth as I scrambled for something to say. It had always been so easy to argue with anyone I ever knew, so why was it so hard to stand up to this old man? It was as if he had some kind of magical power he used to rattle my brain and shake up all my words, forcing me to just play dead. I became fixated on that tone of voice of his, that way of talking that drove me crazy. He didn't yell at me; he didn't even raise his voice. He just had this tone, this way of talking that told me what to do and froze my will to fight back. I finally gave in with a loud "Fine!" and turned to storm out the door. I stopped before I actually went out the door and turned back to face him. "How come you never yell at me?" I asked.

I knew I had caught his attention. Finally, I had at least gotten him to look at me. He gave me a stern look and when our eyes met, I got the strangest feeling. I looked into his eyes and saw two different things: I saw pain, as if I had hurt him or somehow offended him with my question. I also saw something in his eyes that that looked almost like amusement, as if it were the first thing that had made him laugh inside for a long time. I waited for an answer and, as always, I got one. "I'm your grandfather. I don't need to yell for you to listen to me. All I need to do is speak. That should be enough."

He walked right past me and out the door as I stood there thinking about what he had said. I wanted to say it was stupid, that it made no sense. I wanted to pretend that he'd only said it because he didn't have a real answer. I wanted to say he was just a crazy old man who was maybe too tired or weak to yell. I wanted to do anything but admit that he might be right. There was a tiny voice inside of me saying that he had made a point, that he had just given me the reason why he kept getting his way. That voice was telling me I should trust him and listen to him, rather than resent him and fight him. As usual, however, I ignored that voice and refused to listen to it. It was the same voice that told me many times not to fight with the other kids at recess, the same one that had told me to try a little harder in school, and the same one that had told me not to hate my father. More than anything, I hated that little voice because it never went away. I would refuse to listen to it, but I could never get rid of it. I heard it after my grandfather walked by me that day, but as always I turned a deaf ear to it.

I realized my walk to the beach would do no good now so I joined my grandfather on the side of the house. There, he already had the paints, buckets, brushes, and other equipment all set out.

"Do I have to do this, Grampy?" I pleaded. "I'm no good at painting. There has to be something easier I can do. Please?"

"Is that it? You're only good at easy things?" He talked while he finished getting everything ready.

"No, it's not that. It's just that—" He had me. I was stuck. I had no answer.

"I thought so," he said with a little grin. "It isn't that you're only good at the easy stuff: it's just that you don't *want* to do the hard stuff. Right?"

I tried to tell him he was wrong but couldn't. I don't know what was more frustrating, being told what to do or not being able to answer his questions. I wanted so badly to prove he was wrong, but every day that seemed more and more impossible.

"Look, if a seventy-nine-year-old man can paint a house, a healthy ten-year-old boy should be able to do it, too. I'll show you what to do, okay? Watch."

He began to go over the basics of painting with me, but my mind began to wander. I think I was surprised to hear him say he was seventy-nine. When you are ten years old, seventy-nine sounds pretty old, almost ancient. I'd known he was an old man, but I didn't know he was *that* old. It amazed me that he was still so strong. He got around the house and did all his jobs without any problem. I would not have expected a man his age to do that. I always pictured people that old using canes and hobbling around lost and confused. My grandfather was never lost and didn't seem confused about anything. For the first time, I began to think that he seemed younger than he actually was. I had been so focused on seeing him as an "old man" but now that image had started to change. For the briefest moment, I began to admire him for doing so much for someone his age. It was a moment that did not last long, however.

"Hey! Andy! Wake up!" He must have noticed that my mind was drifting away from his painting instructions. He quickly snapped his fingers before my eyes and warned me to stay focused: "You better pay attention or you'll be painting this house twice! Get it?"

"Got it."

"Good." He continued with his directions, showing me how to use everything properly. He modeled how to place the large cloth on the ground so paint would not get on everything it dripped over. He watched me set the stepladder up twice, making sure I did it safely and correctly. He guided my hand as I held the paintbrush, teaching me exactly how much paint should go on the brush and exactly how to stroke it onto the wood. When the painting lesson was over, he showed me the shutters by each window. They also needed to be painted. He went over each step, from taking them off the sea shack, to covering the little nooks and crannies with fresh colors, to putting them back up the way they were. After he got my attention back with his snapping, he had me locked in on every step. I had never been able to pay attention in school. My teachers had tried so hard but I would always let my mind wander off to more important things during class.

Somehow, though, my grandfather must have found that special trick. Whatever he did that day, he got me to listen to everything he said, and I put each lesson into my memory. I wished that my teachers could see me going over the painting lesson with him, learning something new with every piece of instruction.

By the time all his teaching was over, it was almost time for lunch. Grampy went to read his book while I went over in my mind the things he had told me. If I truly was going to paint this house, I wanted to make sure I knew what I was doing. I did *not* want to do the same job twice! I was actually getting excited to start and wished Grampy would hurry up and get done reading so we could start, but, of course, routine was more important and won out. At noon sharp, he made lunch—a turkey sandwich with some corn chips—and I wolfed the meal down in no time. When lunch was over, he went back to read his book.

I kept thinking about the painting lesson and tried to picture myself doing the job. I waited and waited while he read, anxiously anticipating that moment when we would begin working. By this point, I was getting tired of watching him read and finally asked him the latest question that was burning in my mind. "Grampy, why do you read every single day? I mean, wouldn't the painting get done faster if we worked now and put the books away?"

"I thought you'd already know this, Andy: All living things need to eat."

He did it again! Not only did he steal my father's line, but he gave me yet another answer that made no sense. "But...you're not eating: you're reading. I don't get it."

"A turkey sandwich can fill your stomach, but it can't fill your brain. What good is your brain if you never feed it? That's what makes human beings so special, Andy, is our brains. A man who doesn't read is a man who never learns anything, and a man who never learns anything is no better than his dog."

He made a little more sense now, but I was still pretty confused. I didn't want to argue about it, though. I just walked away because I wanted to get the painting project started. His words stuck in my mind, though, as I began the painting job on my own. With each stroke of the brush his answer played over and over again on that radio in my head. As I began my summer job as a painter, I also worked to crack that little riddle he had given me. I felt like I could hear it a million times and still not understand it any better. Eventually, I figured out what he meant; I even came to agree with him. I still wondered why he said things like that, though. Why couldn't he just say he wanted to keep learning new things? Life would be a lot easier, I thought, if he would just tell me exactly what he meant, but I knew he was never going to do that. I'd have to get used to figuring things out on my own.

CHAPTER 8

Time with Grampy moved very slowly. Not much changed around the tiny home. I kept getting up early and even though I hated the idea of working in the summer, I reluctantly did my job painting the house each day. It turned out that it wasn't a two-man project after all: I was the only one painting. He helped me get started and took some time to show me the right way to do things, but after a few days of painting he made himself busy with other projects. I did not say anything, for a change, but I didn't think it was quite fair. When he'd convinced me that I had to do the work, he kept saying we both lived in the house so we both had to paint it. He'd made it sound as if we would be a team working together. Instead, I was alone on the ladder, brushing on a new coat of ivory shine every morning and every afternoon, while Grampy never lifted a brush. I suppose I would have been more upset if he had spent the time relaxing, or reading, or having fun while I worked, but he did other jobs, some of which I could never do. For example, he fixed a pipe in the bathroom that was leaking, and he got an outside shower working again. That way we could wash off any salt or sand that was stuck to us from the beach. He also did all the cooking and cleaning around the house, even the messes I left behind. I knew he was still doing work so I didn't mind him not painting with me.

His doing jobs other than painting also kept him away from me for most of the day. Even though I was doing my best to behave, I was still pretty angry about my summer being ruined. Sure, I was doing my job and maybe I'd started to listen to what he told me, but I still didn't like it one bit. The only good thing about it was that it gave me something to do away from him: As long as I was painting and he was busy with something else, I didn't have to listen to him. He wasn't there to nag me or poke fun at me. He wasn't there to ask me questions or give me useless advice. He simply stayed away from me and left me alone to paint, only stopping by to check on my work now and then. Nothing was going to make my summer get any better. I was still miserable, but, at least while I was painting, I didn't have to deal with him.

It was a warm Thursday afternoon when he came to me, on the ladder painting as usual, and informed me that there was a change in the day's plan. "Finish that section and then come inside. We're low on food and we need to go get some if we're going to eat dinner tonight."

A smile came across my face, and I doubled my working pace, slapping the white paint across the wood siding like an old pro. I finished the small section I was on, washed off my brush, and put the paint away before running inside. The past week had been so slow and boring that the idea of food shopping was like going to the moon. Grampy hadn't taken me anywhere since I'd arrived, and I raced around the old house, preparing to ride in the old truck and, hopefully, to pick out some food I liked from the store. I sprinted through the door and, still wearing a smile across my face, declared that I was ready to go. I should have seen it coming. I should have known things were too good to be true. Once again my grandfather wiped that smile right off my face. When I came into the kitchen, there he was, sitting at the table with a large bucket and two dead fish in front of him.

"Aren't we going to the store to buy food, Grampy?" I asked. I had a gut-wrenching feeling what the answer was going to be, but I had to ask anyway, just to keep my hope alive a second longer before he crushed it.

"No. We don't need the store. We can go there next week and pick up some supplies. Right now all we need is some of this mackerel I keep in the back of the freezer." The fish were frozen stiff. They had a slick, oily look to their skin. I poked at one with my finger and made a face of total disgust.

"We're going to eat those things? You can't be serious. Please tell me we don't have to eat those!"

He let out one of his short, low chuckles. "No, we're not going to eat these." I breathed a sigh of relief before he spoke again, "But our dinner will eat them."

The idea of our dinner, whatever it was, eating these fish erased any appetite I had.

"Why don't we just order pizza, or Chinese food. There has to be something we can have delivered here! Anything!"

He looked at me with raised eyebrows, a quizzical look in his eyes. "You know, Chinese food might be nice tonight. You have money to buy it?"

I didn't even have to say no: I just let my head drop and felt the last gasp of hopeful air seep from my lungs.

"I didn't think so. Now go around back, grab the fishing poles, and meet me down at the beach." As usual, I bottled up the anger and frustration I felt burning inside me and gave in, doing exactly what he had told me to do.

As I carried the rods down the sandy path, I felt the long biting grass graze against my legs. I slunk closer to the water, dragging my feet behind me. The breeze became stronger and cooler against my face as I neared the ocean. This was just plain depressing. I wondered how long I could deal with this. How long could I keep myself from losing control, from telling him how I really felt? How could I keep myself from showing him what a crazy old man he really was? There was probably a pizza place right down the street, but he insisted on living in the Stone Age. A cave man probably would have loved catching his own dinner, but this was not the Stone Age, and I was no cave man. Every inch of my body prayed my grandfather would wake up and join all the normal people in the world. There were easier ways to do things, but he was either too old or too blind to see them. Before my frustrations reached a boiling point, he took the rods from my hand and placed them on the sand by the fish.

"These fish are still too frozen. We'll leave them here to thaw out while we go and get our appetizers." He covered the fish up with a towel and secured it so the seagulls wouldn't fly off with them. Then he picked up the large bucket and ordered me to follow him. We walked along the beach for a while in total silence. My mind dwelt on my misery. We still had no food, and we could have had a piping hot pepperoni pizza on the table by now. I stared at the sand, cursing him with every step for forcing me into yet another of his ridiculous schemes. After we'd walked for a while, he finally broke the silence, explaining in his calm, quiet voice what we were hunting for.

"We're looking for mussels," he said.

That didn't help me much. The only "mussels" I had ever known were the ones in my body, the ones we got all our strength from. Those were *muscles*, though, and I soon learned that my grandfather wasn't talking about those; he was talking about mussels, animals that lived in the ocean. He asked me if I knew what a clam was, and when I told him that I did, he explained that a mussel was like a clam. He taught me that a mussel was a bivalve, which is just a fancy name for a creature with two shells. I learned that clams live in the sand and bury themselves, using a special foot to keep from washing away. He explained that mussels were different because they didn't live on sand, but lived on rocks, wood, or any other hard object underwater.

"If they don't bury themselves in the sand, then why don't they get washed away?" I was still dreaming of my pizza, but he had managed to grab a chunk of my interest without me even noticing it.

"They use a special trick, Andy. Mussels produce a special material, almost like a thick string, and tie themselves down to whatever they live on. These strings are very strong and can hold them tightly in place, even during fierce storms. The mussel's body is narrower than a clam's, and it isn't white. Usually it is blue, black, or gray."

"That must make it hard to see if they live on rocks, huh?"

"You are right on the money, boy. That's why you need to look real hard to see them sometimes. We're in luck though, because I know exactly where to find them." We walked together a little farther until we came to an area where water was rolling over a rocky field. All around us there were small explosions of white water slapping against rocky walls. Once we got closer, we could see hundreds of mussels tied down between the rocks. We walked over to some and Grampy showed me exactly what he had been talking about. He pointed out the two different shells, the strings that tied them down, and I saw how strong they were as he tried to pull a cluster free from its bedding. He finally sprang it loose, pulled each mussel apart from the others, and dropped them into the bucket, one by one.

"Are we using these for bait, too?" This was actually the first moment I stopped thinking about what mussels looked like and began wondering why we needed them.

"No, I told you: these are our appetizers." He flashed me a bright smile, probably because he already knew how disgusted I'd be by eating these things. "Don't worry, you don't eat the shell, just the meat inside. Just like clams. Now help me pull them loose and fill this bucket up." I had eaten clams before at a fish place in Marshfield, and they really weren't that bad. I figured if clams were okay, maybe these would be okay, too. I didn't really want to eat them, but I knew I had no choice, as usual, and thought that maybe I could tolerate them. We would have to see at dinner.

Pulling mussels free from the rocks was more fun than I'd expected. Grampy kept pushing me to grab more, challenging me to gather more than he could. I don't know who reaped more mussels from the rocks, but we filled our bucket up pretty quickly and soon found ourselves walking back to the fishing poles and mackerel. The walk back seemed much shorter than the walk down there and Grampy went off into another lesson the minute we reached the rods.

He cut the thawed mackerel into thick slices and showed me how to put it on the hook. It was high tide by then, and he explained that, during high tide while the sun was going down, was a perfect time to fish. He cast my bait out into the water and showed me how to hold the rod, giving me instructions on what to do if I felt something pull it.

As we sat there, holding the poles, looking out over the water, I listened to his stories of fishing. He made it clear that his best fishing trips were always early in the morning or late at night. As he rambled on about fishing, I got my first glimpse at why he lived here in Truro: He truly loved the ocean. This man, who never went out of his way to talk and rarely seemed interested in conversations with me, began to speak endlessly of his days spent fishing. I once heard that everyone has a passion in life, something that constantly drives them and can get them excited at any moment. It was clear to me that the ocean was Grampy's passion.

I listened to his stories as long as I could before my mind began to drift. We had been sitting there a long time, and the only action was checking the bait every now and again. The bait was still there: the fish were not. Every so often I would feel a small tug and jump up, yelling. "I think I have something!"

"No, you don't," Grampy would say.

"Seriously, it's tugging. I think I have a fish! Should I reel it in?"

"No, leave it alone. You don't have a fish. Trust me, if you get a fish, you will know it for sure." He was speaking so calmly and slowly that you would have thought he was falling asleep. I couldn't blame him, for all the boredom we were sitting through. I knew it was well past his dinnertime, and it was his own fault. I began to wonder if this might teach him a lesson. Would this finally make him open his eyes and live a normal life? He must know that he could have eaten his pizza and watched the news by now if he had done things my way. It was so easy, but he was so stubborn and so old-fashioned. There we were, sitting on the beach with a bucket of mussels and no fish. Dinner was late and it was all his fault. A smile began to crawl across my face as I again began to think, *Victory may finally be mine!* Victory came easy for me with some people, and getting my way was usually a piece of cake. With Grampy, the chances were few and far between. I was certain there was no dinner to be caught, though, and I couldn't wait to point out how wrong he had been when we got back to the kitchen.

I had just started to plan exactly what I would say to him, which words I would use to drive my point through his thick skull, when I got the scare of my life! In a flash my arms were being ripped from their sockets and my body was launched forward. I felt my face hit the sand, and I got a mouthful of tiny rocks. Why I didn't let go of the rod is beyond me, but it seemed like an eternity before I realized what was happening. Grampy grabbed my body and pulled me upright again, helping me keep a grip on the rod. "You got him! You got him!" he screamed directly behind my ears.

I panicked and frantically yelled at him, "Take the rod! Take the rod!"

"No, Andy! He's your fish! Fight him! Reel him in! Fight hard, Andy! That's your dinner out there!" As soon as I realized he wasn't going to reel the beast in for me, I poured all my strength into the rod. I dug my feet deep into the sand to keep the monster from pulling my body forward and did everything my grandfather told me to do. He used his rod to show me how to reel, using my stomach to hold the rod, pulling the tip up as high as possible, then reeling as fast as I could while bringing it down. The bottom of the rod felt like a rock being driven right through my stomach. It pressed harder and harder into me with each pull. Every inch of my arms throbbed in pain as I pulled as if my life depended on it, my hands burning as I struggled to turn that reel, little by little. It seemed like a lifetime that I was fighting that fish, but my grandfather kept cheering me on. He alternated between telling me what to do, and shouting encouragement, telling me he knew I could do it. He was far more excited than I had ever seen him in my life. I wanted that fish for so many reasons. I wanted to prove I was strong enough. I didn't want to lose a fight to a stupid fish that lived in the ocean. The hunger inside my body and the idea that this was my dinner also drove me to battle as hard as I could. I am sure that my grandfather was a major reason, too. I had devoted so much time and energy to trying to get my way that I couldn't let him see me lose. I wondered if he refused to take the rod thinking I would lose the fish, thinking he'd have something to blame on me the rest of the summer. I thought maybe he wanted me to fail so he could use it against me, and I wasn't going to let that happen.

The ferocious battle on the beach raged on. I felt as if I was getting nowhere. Even my grandfather's cheering became slower as he looked into the water, trying to see the fish's movements. I finally got to a point where I wanted to give up, a point where I felt like I had nothing more to give. I heard every cell in my body screaming at me, saying they were exhausted and couldn't do anything more. I was all set to drop the rod and let the fish go, and then I saw it. Just as a wave crashed to the sand, a long flash of silver shot out from the water and danced across my eyes.

"There he is! There he is!" My grandfather raced down to the water, continuing to scream. It was the first glimpse I'd ever had of a fish that size, and it was love at first sight. That silver flash lit a fire inside me, and I forced all those screaming, tortured cells to push forward, just as my grandfather had forced me to go fishing. This extra strength helped me turn that reel a few more times, just enough for Grampy to grab the line in his hands and drag the fish onto the sand. With the monster on land, it was easy to reel and I took in the slack. The fish and I were one, both slumped down in the sand, completely exhausted and gasping for air. I stared at the fish and as soon as I had my energy back, a golden smile lit up my face.

My grandfather stood me up and threw his arms around me. "Aha! There you go, Andy! You are the hero! You are the warrior who is bringing food home to the village tonight!" My prize was a forty-two inch striped bass, a fish that was bigger than I was when Grampy held it up by its gills. It was a stunning fish, with thin black lines running along its body, scales shining bright as the sun let out its very last rays for the day. It was my greatest prize. I was so proud of myself and I could see that Grampy was proud of me, too. He carried the fish back to the kitchen and I followed along, happily swinging the bucket of mussels by my side.

The fishing line had sliced Grampy's hand open when he dragged the bass onto the beach, but he hardly seemed to notice. He simply cleaned himself up in the bathroom, put a bandage over it, and got busy preparing our dinner. Before he did anything with the fish, though, he pulled out his camera and took a few shots of me standing next to it. (One of those pictures still hangs in my room today, and I love telling the story of my first big catch: The day I beat the mighty striper.)

Grampy couldn't stop telling me how proud he was of me while he cleaned and cooked the catch. I suddenly began to realize why he hadn't taken the rod from me. I began to see that he had never wanted me to fail, but that he wanted just the opposite: he'd wanted me to succeed. He loved fishing and knew the thrill that comes with landing a fish. That was a thrill he didn't want to take from his grandson. Slowly, I began to think that maybe he wasn't as bad as I'd thought he was. Maybe I was mistaken in some of the things I had thought about him.

That meal turned out to be the best dinner I had all summer. The mussels were delicious, and the bass, to this day I swear, was the best fish I've ever tasted. I kept eating like a champion, taking more fish until

I couldn't finish the last chunk on my plate. I smiled broadly at Grampy and patted my tummy, wincing a little, having forgotten about the bruise the rod had left there. I got up, walked over to the trash barrel, and scraped the remaining fish off my plate and into the rubbish. I was still licking my chops as I dropped the dirty dish into the sink. As soon as I turned around, I was met by my grandfather's glare.

"Never do that again," he growled at me.

"Never do what again?" He had just spent so much time praising me and telling me how proud he was of me, and now he was upset with me again? "What did I do wrong?"

"I never want to see you throw fish away again. If you put it on your plate, you eat it. Understand?"

"What? Why? We have plenty of fish! What! Do you think we're going to run out?" I opened the door to the freezer and pointed to all the meat he had saved for future meals. "Look at it all! We're fine! Don't worry about the fish. Geez, I'm the one who caught it anyway."

Perhaps my big moment had made me too cocky, and I knew he did not like the tone of my voice. "It's not about how much fish we have, Andy. That bass is a gift, a gift you have to appreciate. You don't take food from nature and throw it away. Okay? Rule number one: If you're going to take it, make sure you use it." This reminded me of our lessons in school about Native Americans, how they made sure they used every part of any buffalo they killed. The only problem was that that was then, and this was now. I was not a Native American and, as far as I knew, neither was my grandfather. I later learned that he actually did have some Native American heritage, but that wasn't the point. The point was that he was ruining my big night. That little voice was back again, the little voice telling me that he was right and that I should listen. It rang out inside of me over and over, a little louder now than it had been before, but again I was able give it my deaf ear. It could get as loud as it wanted: I would never listen.

My mind scrambled again for the best way to fire back at my grandfather. What could I say to prove him wrong? Coming up empty once again, I gave him the only retort that came to mind. "Next time, let's just order pizza. I've had enough of your stupid fishing."

Of course, that wasn't the truth at all. I had loved that moment on the beach, the sight of the giant fish that I had caught and reeled to shore. I would look back on my life in later years and remember that night as one of the best nights of my life, but there was no way I could say that to Grampy. There was no way I could give in. I told myself that the little voice inside of me was dead wrong. I had taken my only shot, insulting the fishing he loved so much, and I stormed off to my bed. As I fell asleep that night, the same old thoughts echoed in my brain. *How long would I be able to survive this? Why had my father done this to me? Why was my grandfather such a stubborn, foolish old man with so many stupid rules?* The only problem was that the questions didn't mean as much to me now. They used to be the kindling that fueled the fire inside of me. Those questions had been what drove me to fight for my own way and not give in to the people around me. I still felt frustrated and angry, but something had changed, I'd begun to feel more frustrated and angry with *myself*. It was as if I was annoyed with myself for asking these questions over and over again. Could it be that I was too hard on him? Could I be wrong about something, or was I being unfair? No, of course not. As I let out more yawns and looked ahead to the early wake-up call, I convinced myself I was just confused and tired. In the morning, I told myself, I would remember why I was so angry at Grampy and my dad. In the morning, the questions would make perfect sense again and prove that I had been right all along. By morning, I would have forgotten about this special night on the beach, and I would renew my campaign to make Grampy leave me alone.

CHAPTER 9

When the wake-up call came at 6:15 the next morning, my entire body was aching. I was so sore from fighting the fish the night before that it hurt just to move from my bed to the floor. I wanted so badly to go back to sleep, but I knew what Grampy would say if I dared to ask. He would say the same thing he had said before, "You'll have plenty of time to sleep when you're gone." I began to think about that. I began to think how nice it would be to go home and sleep as late as I wanted. That day seemed so far away to me but it remained as my light at the end of a very dark tunnel. Grampy did not need to say the words again: I heard them automatically. They forced me to crawl from my cozy bed and out to breakfast.

At breakfast that morning, Grampy managed to surprise me once again. I expected him to say something else about throwing the fish away the night before or respond to my parting comment about ordering pizza. He must have seen me wincing as I moved around, though, or read the expressions on my face, because he didn't say anything about the night before, but simply asked how I felt.

"I feel fine," I mumbled, though of course it wasn't true. But I wasn't going to admit to being weak in front of my grandfather.

"Try again," he said. "And this time, try the truth. How do you feel?"

I had to think for a moment. What was I supposed to say now? Do I lie again and say everything is fine, or do I tell the truth? Do I admit to the pain I am feeling and the purple sores all over my body? I assumed he must have figured it out already or he wouldn't have told me to try again. I slowly groaned back across the table as I chewed my French toast. "I feel like I'm all broken inside, but it is fine. It will go away once I start painting."

Grampy looked me over and then got out of his seat and came over to me. "Stand up, Andy," he said. His voice was unusually soft.

He examined the bruise that was left on my belly and felt the muscles in my arms. He felt along my back and my shoulders, appearing to study every inch of both. I had no idea what he was doing and stood there frozen in confusion. He was looking me over like he was a doctor, but he had never spent a day in medical school. Still, he performed his examination of my bruises and muscles and then delivered his diagnosis.

"You gave yourself quite a workout last night, Andy. No painting today. You need to rest."

Now the old man had completely lost me. No painting? He was so determined to make me work just a week ago, and now he was telling me not to paint but to spend the day resting. I told him again that I was fine and could do the painting. "I don't mind the painting. I want to do it. It's fine. Okay, Grampy?"

"Now you want to paint? Now you want to work? You must have a hard time making up your mind! Didn't you tell me last week that it was too hard for you?"

Was he actually accusing *me* of being confused? Who was he to say that about me! He was the king of confused people! He was the sheriff of Confusion County! I had even wondered if my family called him "Captain" because it was short for "Captain Confusion," not because of his time on the ocean. I stood there staring him down again as these thoughts ran through my head, wondering if I should tell him what I was thinking or keep it to myself. I elected to keep it to myself and simply restated my earlier claim: "I want to paint, okay? I have a job to do and I am going to get it done. End of story." I thought maybe this firm tone would make him listen, but clearly it had no impact.

"No, not 'end of story.' You need to rest today and that's final." This time, however, he took the time to explain his ruling to me. He used a rubber band from a drawer filled with junk to show how my muscles worked. He explained that people did not just become stronger magically, that they actually grew more muscle over time. The more you used the muscle, the quicker it would grow. Apparently, my body hurt so badly because my muscles had been stretched so much while fighting the fish. Just like my father's cell phone, Grampy said, my body only has so much energy and power stored up. If all that energy is used up, the phone needs to rest on a charger until it is powered up to full strength again. Grampy made it clear that these pains meant I was getting stronger, but that my body wouldn't work for me if I used it without enough rest.

Actually, I was not that strongly opposed to the idea of rest. My problem was never with resting, anyway, it was with giving in to my grandfather. In the end, however, I knew he was right, and I agreed to rest for a day. I even took some time to swim in the ocean, believing his advice that it was good for healing the body and the mind. My mind didn't need healing at all, but if anything could help my body feel better, it was worth trying.

The swimming did make me feel a little better, and the pain was going away by dinnertime. The day of rest had done me good, but I couldn't help but wonder what Grampy had planned for me next. I began to fear that this day off would come with price, a price he would be sure to make me pay. That's exactly how miserable this summer had become: even the days off were hard.

CHAPTER 10

As each day passed into each new week, there was one thing I became very good at. It wasn't fishing, swimming, or painting. I wanted to become good at understanding my grandfather, but that wasn't happening either. Of course, I was getting lots of practice with these things, but I wasn't becoming very good at any of them, at least not as fast as I would have liked. What I became a real professional at, though, was keeping everything—all my feelings—to myself. If the ocean was Grampy's passion, then trapping every bitter and angry thought inside of me, keeping it from flying up my throat, was mine. Every morning and every night, Grampy would give me a new reason to despise life in his shack. It may have been about food, or jobs, or the wrong answer, or a silly question, or a careless mistake, or a crazy rule, or anything else the old man used against me. I spent so much time each day thinking of my friends back home and all the fun they were having while I stood in the sun—painting. I could almost see them on their bikes, going through the trails in Marshfield or playing the newest video games and eating whatever snacks they could find. I could see them playing whiffle ball in the yard or street hockey on the pavement. I could see my friends doing all the things I wanted to be doing, all the things I could only dream of doing. They were having the summer every kid is supposed to have while I was stuck in my grandfather's land of misery. Every time I got that picture in my head or a bad thought ran through my mind, I stored it away as quickly as I could, along with the anger I felt toward those who were keeping me from the summer I felt cheated of. Somewhere deep inside me, those images and feelings were put in a chest and locked tightly. I knew it would be wrong to insult my grandfather to his face. I knew I had already done that a few times, but I did not want to make it any worse. There was so much anger and frustration bottled up inside, and it was a struggle to keep it all from pouring out.

It was a struggle that did not last all summer, however. There were times when I let some of it leak out. I complained to my grandfather, for example, when we had a very simple and boring Fourth of July. I wanted so badly to go and see the fireworks at the beach, but we just stayed home and watched a concert on TV instead. That night, I must have told him a million times I wanted to see the fireworks. Little did I know, however, that the fireworks *were* coming. They weren't like the ones in the sky, but that summer, right in the middle of July, the *real* fireworks began to explode.

On that blistering morning in mid-July, the sun was blazing, scorching the land the second it peeped over the horizon. As I stumbled from my bed, I felt as if I were a Thanksgiving turkey roasting in an oven. I stepped outside for only a moment before I felt the scalding rays of fire against my face. It was easily the hottest day of the summer—so hot that my grandfather actually made a change in routine.

As he looked out at the sun and the haze lifting from the shore, he made one of his famous sunrise decisions: "We'll work slow today. It is going to be hot so we need to take it easy. Make sure you drink plenty of water."

"I'm almost done anyway, Grampy. If I don't finish today, I am sure it is going to be done tomorrow." As hard as it was to admit, even to myself, I was starting to feel really proud of my painting. I could see how much nicer it made his home look, and I couldn't deny the sense of satisfaction I got from getting the job done. The past few days he had been telling me it was coming along well. Even when people are full of angry and bitter feelings, they can still feel good about a job well done. On my own, I would never have picked up a brush that summer. Grampy had forced me to do the work, and I was finally starting to feel good about it. Of course, as usual, it took him about three seconds to crush that feeling of joy.

"Almost done, huh? Good, you can start the second coat next week then."

I felt my eyes widen in disbelief and that familiar lump of rage rising in my throat. "Second coat? What do you mean?"

"The second coat, Andy. You do know it needs a second coat to look right, don't you? You always paint twice."

"But...but...you said I'd only have to do it once. Remember? You said—" I groped for words and struggled to stay calm, fighting tears and keeping the words I was truly thinking deep inside. I was becoming so frustrated, sick of feeling this crushing disappointment every time I began to feel good about something.

"I said you would only have to do the job once. Doing the job once means getting both coats done."

"I ha—" I felt the words begin to escape from my body and quickly smothered them with a mumble, stuffing some eggs into my mouth to keep it busy.

"What's that? You have something to say?" He tilted his head so that one eye peered at me intensely while he waited.

My mouth remained set in a firm line as I looked back at him, but inside there was a war raging on. That nagging little voice inside was telling me just to listen to him, to be respectful, and to do what I was supposed to do like a good little grandson. At the same time, all those angry feelings, thoughts, and words were bubbling up like a volcano ready to boil over. I felt the two forces clash inside my heart and when my answer came out, it exploded out of me like a shot from a gun: "No." I angrily pushed my fork back into my eggs and went about eating my breakfast with a scowl.

The annoyance that got my day started sat with me all morning and into the afternoon, much like a bad piece of food that hangs in your stomach for hours. I couldn't shake it, and finally I went down to the water. I hoped that maybe the ocean would help me feel better *inside* this time. Maybe it would help me calm down. At the very least, it would be a break from the heat. I waded out into the water and began to swim about, splashing and swimming harder and harder, steaming mad over the prison I was stuck in. I swam down to a point where there were some large rocks where I could sit and think. Even though I had not confronted my grandfather that morning, I could still feel that battle being fought within my own body: It was the little voice against all the bad things I was feeling, and as annoying as the voice had always been for me, I was hoping it would win this one time. I was truly afraid of how hard life would be if I let the anger win and told him how I really felt.

Once I had rested a bit and calmed myself down, I got up from the rocks to swim back. As if the day had not been bad enough, my bathing suit tore as I got up. It had become caught in a crack between two rocks, and the whole back of the leg tore open when I moved forward. I let out a loud sigh of frustration as I looked back to see how big the tear was. I realized my only luck was that the tear didn't go too high up and really embarrass me. Fortunately, I was able to swim back to the sea shack without people noticing the tear. I changed and threw the bathing suit into the trash, disgusted with this entirely terrible day.

It was about an hour later when my grandfather came back inside for some water. He stopped in his tracks when he saw the bathing suit. "What's this?" He had a deeply inquisitive tone to his voice and gave me a curious look.

"It ripped while I was swimming today. I got it caught on the rocks. I guess I'll need to go into town and find a new bathing suit tomorrow."

Grampy did not say anything. He just gave a quiet grunt as he studied the tear from several different angles. I was drinking my water and watching some TV, so I did not notice that he took the ruined suit into his room. I'm not even sure how long he was in there before he came back out and threw the bathing suit over to me. "Good as new," he said, as he reached for the ice cold water in the fridge.

Confused as usual, I picked up the bathing suit and immediately noticed a large red stripe in the back that had not been there before. It was really ugly, especially since the rest of my bathing suit was blue. I looked at that stripe in the same strange way he had looked at the tear before. I was getting hot inside, and knew I couldn't let this go. "What? This isn't *good as new*? It's *ruined*!"

"You can swim in it, right? Just like a new bathing suit? It's good as new, only free." He began to drink his water and calmly looked out the window, as if he weren't bothered at all by my protest.

"Are you listening to me? I can't swim in this! I'll look like an idiot with this big stupid stripe down my leg! Didn't you hear me when I said we'd have to get a new one?"

"Yes, I heard you, but you are wrong. You don't need to spend money for something new when you can fix the old. That is *your* bathing suit and you *will* swim in it. Understood?"

His commanding eyes locked on to mine. And that's when it happened. That is the moment I lost all control and completely fell apart. It was one of those moments you can see coming, want so badly to stop, but realize it's already happening before you can do anything to stop it. The volcano was erupting and I felt that little voice inside of me being drowned in a raging river of red-hot emotional lava. It blew out of my heart, burned through my stomach, shot up through my throat, and finally came out of my mouth with a roar.

"NO! NO! I hate you! I want a new bathing suit! I don't want your stupid red stripe on my leg! I don't even want to be here! You're just an old man who doesn't have a clue and I hate living with you! Don't you get it? Everything you do is just so stupid and so crazy and, and—"

There must have been a traffic jam of angry words trying to get out of me, because I suddenly stumbled over what to say next and simply waved my hands in the air, my mouth wide open.

He began to talk but this time *I* was the one interrupting *him*. "Stop talking! Okay! Stop! Stop telling me what to do and stop ruining my life! Don't act like you're my boss, okay? Because you're not! You're just an old nobody, and you can't push me around! Can't you see that? Why can't you just stay away from me? I don't want anything to do with you! I don't even want you in my life! Just live in this crummy, stupid, ugly, little shack all by yourself, paint your own stupid home, catch your own dumb fish, fix your own nasty clothes, and leave me the hell alone!"

The room became deadly silent. We stared at each other. I was angry, terribly angry, but I was also shocked at what I had just said. The little voice began to come back as I caught my breath from all the shouting, and I could hear it faintly scolding me: "Shame on you, Andy. Shame on you."

I knew I'd better brace myself. I knew I had to prepare for whatever my grandfather was about to do. I didn't think he'd hit me, but whatever he did to me, I knew it would hurt. If I had learned anything, it was that Grampy could fire back at anything I threw his way. Despite what I said about him being an old nobody, I knew in my heart that he was a man of power and a man with authority. I knew he would make me pay for all the things I had just screamed at the top of my lungs. He would take his revenge, for sure, and I got ready for a harsh and painful lesson in manners.

I stood there, panting and waiting, waiting and worrying, preparing for the very worst. After a few nervous moments, I looked him right in the eye and saw something that almost knocked me to my feet: I saw a tear. I'll never forget seeing that, the tiny drop of water building up in the corner of his right eye and then slowly working its way down his rough, wrinkled cheek. I watched that lonely tear run down his weathered face—and then I watched him walk out the front door without saying a word.

CHAPTER 11

After my blowout with Grampy, after watching him walk out of the sea shack, I felt a tear roll down my cheek. That tear opened the floodgates to my sorrow and pain. I ran to my bed and buried my face in the pillow, sobbing so much I could feel the bed becoming wet from the tears. I tried to think about what would happen now, but I couldn't even imagine it. I knew I had done something horrible. I knew it was terrible to say those things to my grandfather, and I knew it would not make my stay there any better. He'd surely make me work harder, create stricter rules, and make everything more difficult for me. He would make me pay for all the things I had said to him. Life there had been so hard for me, so difficult, and the idea of it becoming that much worse was unbearable. I kept crying and sobbing on that pillow, thinking that at any moment he would come home. I kept waiting to hear the door open, to hear his footsteps walking into the kitchen.

Those sounds did not come. I had not heard any sign of him coming home. The only sounds were my weak sobs, the chirping crickets outside, and the distant waves crashing along the beach.

Whenever someone spends enough time crying, the tears eventually must stop. Sometimes a person just feels better and doesn't need to cry any more, and sometimes it is almost as if the eyes run dry, and there are simply no more tears to shed. That is what happened to me that night. I still hurt inside and could not stop thinking about what I'd said to Grampy, but I had simply run out of tears and finally stopped crying.

He still had not come home, and I began to wonder where he had gone. His old truck was still in the driveway, so he could not have been too far away. Suddenly, I thought maybe he had come home and I just hadn't heard him. Perhaps I was just so upset and too busy crying and had missed his return to the shack. I slowly walked out of my room and peered around the dividing wall into his. It was completely empty, I had not missed him, he simply wasn't here. Where could he have gone?

I wondered if I should go out and look for him. If anything bad happened to him, I knew I would feel worse and think it was all my fault. He was sturdy and strong for his age, but he was still an old man and anything could happen. My father had always told me that nobody ever plans on having an accident, and I began to worry that maybe one had happened to Grampy. I thought about going out to search for him, but I didn't even go near the door. It was too dark and I was sure I would get lost on my own. Instead, I did something I had not dared to do all summer: I went into his room. He had never told me to stay out of his room, and he'd never said anything that made me afraid to go in there, but for some reason I had always stayed away from it. This was the first time I had set foot inside it. An eerie feeling came over me as I walked towards the door to his room, almost as if a magnet inside of me was drawing me towards that doorway. I was strangely nervous about what I might see in his room and yet I was also incredibly curious.

All the rooms in his little sea shack were so small that he couldn't fit very much into his space. His bedroom was no different. His bed against the wall was flanked on each side by a small table. One had a little clock on it and a lamp, the other some old pictures. To my left as I walked in, there was an old chest tucked into the wall. The chest had drawers down low where he kept his clothes, and I could tell the top opened up to a big space inside. He had a few shirts on top of the chest, and some blankets on the shelf up above it. That was also where he kept his flag. What I had not noticed before and what amazed me the most was a wall that was covered with different pictures, certificates, and letters. He looked so young in all the pictures, yet much the same as he did now. The biggest difference was that his hair was as black as coal in the pictures, and his skin had fewer wrinkles in it. In some of the photos he was on a boat or near the beach with other guys just like him—probably his friends. Many other pictures showed him wearing an army uniform, and standing by tanks and airplanes, or carrying a large machine gun in his hands. In some of the pictures, he stood with other men wearing the same uniform. I began to realize that my grandfather must have been in a war when he was younger. The other men must have been the people he had fought with. I began to put the puzzle pieces together in my mind, slowly learning more details about my grandfather's life. No wonder he was so tough on me. I had learned from TV and the movies just how hard life was in the army. I was coming to understand that he must have learned to be so strict and tough with every little rule while he was a soldier.

I don't know how long I stood entranced, staring in awe at the pictures in his room. I hadn't heard a sound, hadn't heard a door open, hadn't heard his footsteps, but as if out of nowhere, I heard someone behind me. I swallowed hard under the shadow his body cast over mine and heard him say in a low, crackly voice "Were you looking for something?"

"No, Grampy. I wasn't." My voice was just louder than a whisper, and, unable to bring myself to look him in the eyes, I kept my head tilted to the floor. "I'm sorry. I didn't know if you were coming back. I was just looking around. I didn't touch anything, I swear, okay? I was just looking around: that's all."

"Relax, you didn't do anything wrong. Nobody said you couldn't come in here." He took off his shoes and sat on his bed, slumping his body forward as if he were completely exhausted. The room was filled with the worst silence I had ever felt. Should *I* say something? Was *he* going to say something? Should I just go to bed? What was he thinking? Seconds seemed like hours until I finally spoke a few more timid words.

"Y—you were in a war? Grampy? Are those pictures from war?"

"Yes, I was in a war." He kept to his short and simple style, despite our fireworks display of a few hours back.

"What war?" I was genuinely curious, but afraid he would think I was just acting like nothing had hap-

118

pened between us. I didn't want him to think I was just pretending to be interested.

He took a moment to think, looking over at me, his eyes questioning me, as if he was trying to figure out why I suddenly cared about this. I felt as if he was examining me to see if it was worth talking to me any longer. If that really was what the questioning look meant, I must have passed the test, because he answered me. "World War II and Korea, Andy. Both of them."

Surprised, I moved closer to him and added some volume to my voice. "Both of them? You had to fight in two wars?"

I could tell he was tired and thinking of sleep, but he talked on. "Ohhh, I probably didn't have to go to Korea, but I went anyway. My country said they needed me, and I was happy to go along."

I could not imagine going to fight in one war, never mind two of them. I thought soldiers back then were all *made* to fight. It puzzled me that my grandfather could have chosen to stay home and be safe but had decided to go and fight in a second war. "You must have liked fighting a lot then, huh?"

He sighed heavily. "Liked fighting? No, none of us liked fighting. I like my country, though. Wait, make that I *love* my country. We were proud to fight for her. Someday you'll understand, Andy."

I *began* to understand that night. It was probably one of the most meaningful moments in my life, that moment in July when I began to change. It was the moment I finally began to understand. It was as if a fiery lightning bolt had shot through my entire body, pushing my eyes wide open and making me finally wake up. I had been so focused on being miserable all summer long that I never took the time to really see who my grandfather was. He was still the same man, but in my eyes everything about him was altered that night. I not only began to see how great he was for being an American soldier, but I also began to see how great he was as a regular person. His rules began to make sense. His routines began to have a meaning and a purpose to them. His way of life no longer seemed entirely boring and mind numbing to me, but it began to seem, well, beautiful. Part of me became filled with excitement, curiosity, and wonder about who this man really was and what else I could learn about him. A bigger part of me, however, felt ashamed. As I began to see that he was someone really special, I felt the guilt growing deep inside of me.

"Grampy?" My voice sounded uncertain, as if I didn't really expect an answer. I thought maybe he would ignore me, but he didn't.

"Yes? What now?" He was laying on his back now, his eyes closed tight. He sounded very tired, but I knew he was listening.

"Umm—well, I—ummm—," I don't think I could have counted all the emotions running through me at that moment, everything from fear to shame, and it all made talking more difficult than it had been all summer.

"Spit it out, Andy! A man needs to say what he means and mean what he says, so let's hear it."

"I'm sorry." Two simple words, but two words that were so hard to get out that night. Two words that held the key to releasing so much of my guilt, and two words that carried the hope of making us friends again. "I shouldn't have said those things to you. I didn't mean them, okay? Can you forgive me?"

"Of course I can forgive you, Andy: you're my grandson. Now go to bed and sleep it off. We've both had a long night."

"I really am sorry. I didn't mean any of it, okay?" The man had just said he would forgive me, but I guess I wasn't quite done getting my guilt out. It was as if his forgiveness wasn't the only thing I needed, that hearing myself apologize again was just as important. "I know I hurt you and it was wrong. I should have been a lot nicer and not made you cry like that."

His eyes slowly shot open, and he looked directly at me with a very serious, thoughtful look. It was that look a person has when he wants to say something, but is not sure if he should or not. "What you said didn't hurt me: it didn't make me cry," he said softly, "Now go to bed."

Of course, I could have just gone to bed and let it go, but I persisted with my questions because I knew I had seen him crying. Back home, my father always told me there was nothing wrong with crying some-times, and I wasn't going to let my grandfather say he didn't cry when I knew he did. "I saw you, though. You started crying before you left."

"Yes, I know," he finally admitted. "I was cry-ing, but not because of what you said to me. Believe me, boy, I have had a lot worse said to me in my seven-ty-nine years and I didn't cry those times either."

"Then why were you crying? If it wasn't what I said, what was it?" I couldn't let this go. It was an an-swer I needed to know. Before, I would have wanted to know so I could maybe use it against him down the road, but it was different now. This time it was about understanding him and learning from him, not setting him up for revenge.

Again, he took a long pause before speaking. "You just reminded me of someone I once knew, okay? Now I mean it, Andy: get to bed! It's too late for this and you need your sleep."

Confusion set in, and I didn't get an inch closer to my bed. "Reminded you of someone? Who? Who did I remind you of, Grampy? Who was it?" I needed to know this answer before I even thought of sleep, and I relied on the old kid trick of asking over and over until you get what you want. I asked and asked again, dodging his attempts to get around the topic and get me to bed, asking until he finally caved in and told me.

"Your mother. You reminded me of your mother." The mouth that had been firing an array of questions five seconds ago hung wide open in total surprise now. My mother? It was not what I was expecting, not even close to it. I reminded him of my mother? *Me?* He had already rolled over and turned his lamp off, a signal that the conversation was over for sure now.

It took me a good long time to move, but I slowly dragged my feet to my bed, still puzzled by what he had said. I didn't understand how my being so mean to him, so unfair with him and so loud, could have possibly reminded him of my mother. It didn't make sense to me. I went to bed then: I had no choice. But I was determined to get more answers in the morning. I don't think I slept a wink that night, kept awake by the new eyes through which I now saw Grampy, and thinking about my mother more than I ever had before.

CHAPTER 12

There is an old saying that goes "Today is the first day of the rest of your life." For most people on most days, that's all it is—just a saying, one of those things they say but don't really mean. When I hopped out of bed the next morning, though, it truly was the first day of the rest of my life. As I walked out to breakfast, it was like walking into a new beginning. I can look back now and see all the things that changed after that night with Grampy, but that morning I didn't know what was coming. I did not know exactly what would happen in my future, but I had a different feeling inside me. I thought that maybe things would actually get better with Grampy. I wasn't sure of that, but at the very least, I was, for the first time since I'd arrived, looking forward to seeing him.

I wanted to know what he had meant by my reminding him of my mother, but I also didn't want to push his nerves. I was afraid if I brought it up first thing in the morning, it might upset him or make him uncomfortable. I kept telling myself to wait until later, at least until the afternoon when he was done with his work and ready to relax. I must have told myself a thousand times not to bring it up, but my effort only lasted about ten minutes. I broke the regular routine of breakfast by quickly delivering the burning question in a loud voice: "Grampy? How did I remind you of my mother?"

"Oh, lots of ways," was all he said.

I smiled at the short, direct answer. The smile was a sign that I was starting to appreciate him. The same style of conversation that had annoyed me so much these past few weeks began to seem sort of charming to me. I felt glad that he kept his style and didn't change, even after our fight, but I still wasn't satisfied with his answer.

"But how? I mean, what exactly reminds you of her?"

"Everything."

I had learned by then that, when dealing with Grampy, it usually took three tries to get the answer I wanted. It was almost like baseball, when the pitcher has to throw three strikes in order to reach his goal. He would later reveal to me that there was a method to his madness, saying if something is not important, you won't ask about it a third time. This was most definitely important enough to ask a third time: "But what? Can't you tell me something specific?"

He put down his fork and looked across the table with a smile. It was a smile that took him back in time, back to when he was raising a family. "Your face...your eyes...your nose.... You look just like her. The way you walk and talk—just like her. Even last night, the way you got so mad and started shouting and screaming. It was like hearing her all over again, yelling at me because she couldn't go out late or couldn't get the things she wanted. Everything about you reminds me of your mother."

"You must really miss her then...since it made you cry."

"Yes, I do. People cry for lots of reasons, though, Andy. People cry because they are sad, and sometimes they cry because of love. Sometimes both."

"Is that why you cried last night? Because of both?"

"Yes, Andy, I suppose that is why. I loved your mother so much. She was my only daughter, and…well…she was very special to me."

I could tell he was starting to feel a little emotional again as he took his mind back over the years, and I put my questioning on pause for the moment. As I slowly ate my eggs, I used the quiet time to think over what he had just said. It was the most he had revealed about himself since I had come here, and I was happy knowing that he would tell me these things. I felt funny asking about my mother and hearing stories about her but, at the same time, I was also excited, thirsting for more and looking to go deeper. As a young child, I was never very good at keeping a silence, and so another question popped out of me. "Were you angry that she died?"

"Angry? At who?"

"I don't know. Ummm....angry at God, I guess."

He smiled again and let out one of his famous low chuckles. "No, I wasn't angry at God. As you get older, Andy, you learn a lot of things. One thing you learn is that sometimes bad things happen and there is no explanation or anyone to blame. It's simply a part of life you learn to understand with time...or at least try to understand."

Just as I was beginning to work that idea over in my mind, the hammer of a rapid knock sounded at the door, and I jumped up to open it. An older woman who looked to be around Grampy's age stood in the doorway, glancing nervously over her shoulder towards the beach every few seconds. Grampy wiped his mouth, slowly rose from his chair, and stepped over to the door to greet her.

"Can I help you with something, Rose?" Clearly, he knew this woman and didn't seem to mind her knocking on the door so early in the morning.

"Yes, you can. Well...at least...I think you can...I hope..." It was easy to see that she was very worried about something. She continued on as she tried to catch her breath. "Down on the beach. There's a gull that's caught up in some fishing line. He can't open his mouth or even fly. I figured, or I was hoping, that maybe you could do something to help it?"

Without hesitation, Grampy strode out the door. He turned with a stern look on his face to give me my orders: "Andy, get my pliers and gloves out of the kitchen drawer and follow me down to the beach."

I bounded into the kitchen and found the drawer. I grabbed the gloves and pliers, turned around, and quickly sprinted out the door as fast as I could to catch up. Maybe it was just a seagull, but it was the most exciting thing to happen around here for a while. Just seeing another person was exciting, since Grampy almost never had visitors. On our way down to the beach, the woman apologized over and over to Grampy for bothering him so early. He simply told her over and over not to worry about it. When we got to the beach, we saw the seagull right away. He was a ways down the shore from Grampy's shack, but you could just make him out, flailing and flopping around helplessly in the sand.

"I was out for my morning walk when I came across him. Oh, I hope he is okay. You can help him, right?" She was still very worried and kept putting her hand up to her mouth, but she seemed to believe in my grandfather very much. Once we reached the bird, she and I stayed a few feet away from it while Grampy put the gloves on and began to look at it as closely as he could.

"These dang fishermen! They come down here and leave all their trash hanging around!" He had a slightly angry tone in his voice now, and he swung his head towards me, pointing a finger. "You better swear to me, Andy, as long as you fish, you better keep all your trash off the beach!" He didn't wait for an answer and just went back to examining the bird, carefully and slowly circling around it. "These idiots think they own the beach and don't even care if they're destroying it."

By that point, my heart really was going out to the bird. At first, I hadn't wanted anything to do with it as I looked at his sharp beak, his jagged little claws, and that mean glare in his eyes. He clearly needed help, but he was also warning me to stay away from him. Every time he tried to stand, though, he quickly fell over. Part of the fishing line had wrapped around his body so he couldn't use his wings or his right leg. The rest of the line was wrapped tight around his beak. I could tell he wanted to screech and caw at the strangers around him, but he couldn't open his beak enough to peep. He was trapped, unable to walk, fly, eat, or even make noise, and he was probably terrified.

Suddenly, Grampy made his move and leaned forward over of the bird, holding its body and neck tight in his hands. "Quick, Andy! Take those pliers and cut this line off."

"Me? But...but...." Those claws and the beak still looked pretty scary to me, even if the bird was in trouble.

"Now, Andy! You need to help him! Let's go!" It was the closest thing to a yell that Grampy had given me all summer, and it told me he meant business. The lady kept watching intently, her hand over her mouth, while I timidly approached the bird with the pliers in my hand.

"Cut the line around his wings and legs first so he can't bite you."

If Grampy had not been able to hold the bird so tightly, my job would have been a lot tougher, but he had a firm grip on the creature while I carefully clipped the line away from the wings and feet. "Now what, Grampy?"

"Now take the pliers and get as much of that line around his beak as you can. Cut the line so his beak is just barely free. He'll do the rest while we get away."

The bird's head was moving much more than his body, so this part was much trickier. With a little fumbling, though, I maneuvered my shaking hands so that the pliers had a good grip on most of the line. I cut it and saw most of the mess come loose. Grampy nodded to me, letting me know it was good enough, and I scurried away as quickly as I could. Next, he released the gull and took a few long strides backwards, making sure that he, too, was at a safe distance.

The three of us watched and waited as the bird struggled and kicked a little more. Within a few seconds, his powerful wings began to push the fishing line away from his body and his leg came loose from the tangle. With a running start, he flapped his wings and took off from the sand, shaking the last bits of line from his beak and letting out a continuous chorus of caws as he flew high above us. In a way, it seemed like he was thanking us, and as I helped Grampy and his friend Rose pick up the fishing line, I reveled in the warm feeling of having done a good deed. "Rose, I'd like you to meet my grandson, Andy O'Brien." He smiled as he patted me on the back and she stretched her hand out to shake mine.

"Well, it's a pleasure to meet you, young man. I'm Rose Hewitt, an old friend of your grandmother's. Are you staying with your grandfather long?"

"Yeah, the whole summer. My dad had to go away on business, so I'm staying down here." It was funny, because it was the first time I'd said that without using a word like "stuck," "ruined," or "stupid." I didn't even say it with the same attitude I'd had before.

"Well, you're a lucky boy, then. I live a little ways down the beach, down that way, in a white cottage. You'll know my house because there is a flag outside with a goose on it." She laughed to herself, apparently thinking there was something funny about the goose flag. "Anytime you need anything, Andy, you come down and see me. Any grandson of Dootie's is certainly a friend of mine!"

I tried to keep myself from laughing and looked at my grandfather, wondering if I should say it. "Dootie?"

He gave me a look that told me it was the last time *I* would ever use that name. "It's a nickname. Your grandmother used to call me that. *You* can call me Grampy. Got it?"

I shrugged. "Yes, Grampy," I said. I had to turn away to hide my smirk, but I couldn't stop the giggle that escaped me as I looked down the beach.

"Well, I need to get running along back home. It was nice to meet you, though, Andy!"

"Nice to meet you too, Mrs. Hewitt." She turned and walked towards her home, while Grampy and I turned to walk back to the shack. There wasn't much said as we marched along in the sand, but once we got back near the sand dunes in front of his home, I asked him about what had just happened.

"Why did you go to help that bird so quickly, Grampy? I mean, you could have been bit or clawed by him. You didn't know what he was going to do."

He stopped alongside me and began to look up and down the shore. "Andy, look around. What do you see?"

I took a quick glance before my eyes came back to him. "A beach. Why?"

"No, look closer. What is it that we have all around us? Look at *everything*."

I tried to look closer, and his questions took me back to my science lessons in school. I did notice more than before, but I wasn't too certain what the correct answer was. I took another shot: "Nature?"

"Yes, Andy, this is nature...all of it. And like it or not, *you* are a part of it. Just like the seagull, or the fish or the cricket, you are an animal and part of nature. You know what the first rule of nature is, Andy?"

I made it look like I was coming up with an answer, but I had absolutely no clue and finally gave in. "No. What is it?"

"Everything takes care of everything else. Each little plant and animal has its own special place, its own special job. Go ahead, name an animal, and I can tell you its place in nature, its special job."

This seemed like a stupid game, but I played along. "A crab."

"A crab? Well, the crab eats dead fish and some even eat plants so we don't get too many of either one. But, the crab is also food for some fish so they can grow and be healthy. Try another one?"

"Whales."

"Oh, that's an easy one, Andy! See, there are tiny animals in the water called plankton and krill, and the whales around here eat them. If they didn't eat them, the water would be too cloudy, no light would get in, plants would die, and all the other animals would start to die off, too."

I was starting to get into the game a little more now, and I searched around the beach for something that would be sure to stump him. "Ah, okay, I've got it. What about all this grass? All it does is sting your legs and annoy you when you walk in it. What good is that?"

His smile told me right away he had another answer. "Come with me."

I followed him as he slowly stalked his way into the grass. After a little searching, he waved his hand, signaling me to come forward. Pushing the grass apart, he pointed out where some sort of nest had been. "You see, Andy, a bird made its nest here, hatched its eggs, and raised its young. It could only do that because the grass hid the nest so well. Predators couldn't see the nest, so they were safe." He led me out of the grass and up to the top of a sand dune as he continued to teach me about nature. "It's like I said, Andy. Everything has a place and a job—including you. Sometimes that means not leaving your trash behind, sometimes it means not wasting valuable fish from the sea, some-times it may mean feeding the birds in your yard, and sometimes it may even mean helping out a seagull in trouble. Look around, Andy, and you'll see how beauti-ful nature really is."

This was the third time he had told me to scan the horizon around me. The first two times I hadn't seen much, but this time something clicked. I was able to see how everything—from the clouds and sky, to the ocean, to the sand and the grass—fit together in one perfect picture. I had an idea of how every little animal, even me, had its own piece in this picture. It was all coming together, and it was absolutely amazing.

Grampy was silent, not so much because he wanted to stay on the dune but because he could see the wonder in my eyes. He could tell he was making sense to me right now and that this was something important. He didn't say anything more but slowly turned and began walking back to the sea shack. I turned and watched him lumber back through the grass and I smiled. Something had, in fact, changed. A day ago I couldn't stand him, and now I was starting to admire him. I thought about how confident Mrs. Hewitt was in him, about the pictures hanging on his wall, about the little lessons he had been trying to teach me. Despite his rules and chores, I thought about how nice he had actually been to me since I had arrived there...and I took off running after him.

I called out to him, "Are you going to the garden now, Grampy?"

His response was low, and I could just barely make it out since he didn't bother to turn towards me. "Nope. I think I need to put the flag out first."

I ran through the grass, not even noticing the tiny bites as they flicked against my legs. "Wait! Wait for me! Hold up, Grampy!" He stopped and turned to me, showing a look that clearly had "What now?" written across it.

Still feeling guilty for having been so mean to him, I hoped to do something that might make up for it. "I want to do it," I panted as I finally caught up to him.

I took some small satisfaction in the look of surprise on his face. It was not an angry surprise or a disappointed surprise, but a very happy surprise. "What? You want to raise the flag?"

"Yes, I do. I want you to show me how to do it so I can raise it in the mornings and take it in at night. I mean, if it is okay with you."

It was one of the brightest smiles I had seen on him yet, one of those smiles that warms your whole body and lets you know you've made someone else happy. "Yeah, it's okay with me. Come on, I'll show you what to do."

I, too, could not stop smiling as Grampy showed me how to raise the flag and explained every detail about handling it. It was very clear that the flag was important to him, and I think he was proud of me for wanting this job. He taught me what each color and symbol meant. Red stood for courage and strength, white was purity and innocence, and blue stood for justice. The thirteen stripes were to remind us of the thirteen original colonies our country started with. Grampy also showed me how to keep the flag from touching the ground and how to fold it the right way every time. Even each fold had its own special meaning. The first fold, for example, was a symbol of life, and the other folds recognized people such as our soldiers, even our mothers and fathers who cared for us. Some stories about the flag surprised me. I had always seen people salute the flag, but I'd never known that the first people to salute it were the French. One of our war ships was in France in 1778, and all the French sailors stopped to salute the flag sailing by. I was learning from the master, and I was honestly enjoying it. In one morning he had helped me understand nature better than anyone else ever had before. He helped me start to fall in love with the beautiful world that was around me every day. Finally, he had helped me understand and care for the symbol of our country, the country he risked his life for in war. The first day of the rest of my life was going great, and it was still only morning.

CHAPTER 13

The rest of that day—and the rest of the week, for that matter—was one of the best rides I had ever experienced. It was as if I had been standing still all summer and suddenly took off like a jet, learning new things more quickly than I could have imagined. Aside from teaching me about nature and the flag, Grampy began teaching me other things. Some of these were chores around the house, such as fixing things with small breaks in them or cleaning things so well that you would swear they were new. I got through these lessons just fine, but there were some that I truly enjoyed and had never even thought about learning before.

Of all the things Grampy took the time to show me, cooking is the one I may use the most today. So many people had always told me to stay away from the stove, not to touch the pans, to be careful around the pots, and basically not to even think about doing anything cooking related. I suppose when you are a kid who gets into trouble often, people are nervous about letting you use dangerous things like a stove. Grampy didn't see things that way, though. One of his many gifts that he gave me was his willingness to give me a chance. While all the other people in my life were trying to keep me out of trouble, Grampy was the one who pushed me to prove I could do better.

When the idea of cooking first came up, I told him people didn't let me use the stove because they thought I would either hurt myself or cause a fire, but that didn't bother him. I'll never forget hearing him say, "A stove is perfectly safe if you use it responsibly. Can you do that?" Believe it or not, I actually had to think about that question for a moment but, of course, I wasn't going to say no! My first cooking lesson was an easy one: how to make a grilled cheese sandwich. Easy, but critically important since it was one of my very favorite foods. I figured that once I learned how to cook grilled cheese, I was set for life. I could eat those sandwiches all day long and all night, too!

As usual, Grampy had a riddle to go along with this first cooking lesson. He watched me carefully as I built my sandwich, using two beautiful slices of American cheese. "You see, Andy, if you give a man some fish, he will eat for a day. But if you teach a man to catch fish, he can eat for his entire life." I am not even sure I should simply call it a "riddle": it was more than a word game. It was a game with a lesson. He used those sayings to make what we were doing a little more interesting but also to explain to me *why* I was learning the lesson.

"I get it, Grampy." When I could respond to his riddles now, it filled me with a proud energy, knowing that we were connecting on the same idea. "It's like...if I love eating pizza down at Papa Gino's, I can go down there and get a meal. I need a car and money to get the pizza though. But if I learn to make pizza the way I like it, I could be at home and eat it anytime I wanted. Right?"

"Yeah, you get the idea." He said this with one of those wonderful chuckles and a smile to match it. I think he was having fun with my explanations. If he mentioned fish, I talked about pizza. If he said truck, I'd say a car. If he talked about vegetables, I would talk about candy. It was a fun way for us to say the same thing in our own way. When I had wanted to order pizza before and we'd had our fight, I'd wondered if it was an anti-pizza thing, if he just hated pizza for whatever reason. I felt convinced he did not approve of my liking pizza. Now I knew that pizza had nothing to do with it. He didn't care if I talked about pizza, candy, cars, or rockets, for that matter: he just wanted to be sure I was getting the message, and I was.

In a way, learning to cook was the same lesson as mending my torn clothes. He also taught me how to clean up cuts when I got them outside, and how to get rid of things like headaches and a sore throat without using medicine. I was beginning to see the truth behind these lessons. There was plain, solid good sense in everything he did. He did not do things for any of the silly reasons I had thought of before. It was not that he was too cheap to buy new clothes or pay for headache medicine. It was not that he was too lazy to go shopping. He simply believed that people should take care of themselves as much as they could. True, he had his own unique way of doing things, but what really and truly made his methods so special, was that they usually worked better than anything I had ever tried before.

It was an especially warm night when I brought this up to him, during another fishing trip under the stars. "You seem like you don't need anybody, Grampy. You fix all your clothes; you cook all your food yourself; you even catch most of it. Instead of going to a doctor or a nurse, you work on your own cuts. It's like you can do everything on your own and never need anybody else. That is so cool."

I heard it again, the low chuckle. The night was dark, but once I heard my grandfather's chuckle, I didn't need to see his face: I knew the smile was there too.

"It's not so much that I don't need anybody, Andy: it's just important to be able to do things yourself. I still go to the doctor, and I will still buy clothes from a store, but only if I need them and it is a good deal. I get plenty of food from the market still, and there are some other things I can only get from other people. But part of being an adult is being able to take care of yourself and not going to other people for *everything*."

I have no idea why I said what I said to him next. It was another one of those things that came shooting out before I could stop it in my throat or even take time to think about. I know it came from somewhere, and it must have been somewhere deep because, in a way, I felt terribly sad after I'd said it. "Do you need *me*, Grampy?"

He put down his fishing pole and slid in the sand closer to me. I saw him appear out of the darkness and place a hand on my shoulder. "What do you think, Andy?"

I lowered my head, and tears began to run down my face. Where was this coming from? What was happening? I softly muttered my answer: "No." When I said that, the floodgates opened and I began to build a river in the sand with my tears.

Grampy gave me a firm yet very tender hug. He was a man who rarely gave anyone a hug. It surprised me. Then, he looked me straight in the eyes and used that firm voice I swore he must have found in the army somewhere. "If you really believe that, Andy, you still have a lot to learn. You should know better by now."

"So...you...you *do* need me?" I still wasn't totally sure.

"Yes, Andy, I need you very much. Lots of people need you." He let go of my shoulders and turned back to his rod for a moment, but it still felt like he was holding me somehow. I sniffled loudly and wiped at my tears. "But you can do everything, Grampy. What do you need me for? You've been teaching me everything, but it is all stuff you can do by yourself."

His eyes locked into mine again, and the firm voice returned. He spoke to me the same way my teachers did when they knew I hadn't been listening in class, but this time it really sank in.

"Andy, listen to me! You are right. I don't need you here to do all the work. I can paint on my own, I can raise and lower the flag on my own, I can cook for myself, and I can catch my own fish. But you give me more than that. You are my grandson, and I need you because you give me more than anyone else can."

"Like what?" I think the whiny tone of my voice was starting to annoy him just a bit.

"I guess you just haven't been paying attention," he said as he turned away, giving me a moment to think.

"Paying attention to what?"

Grampy picked up his rod and began walking back to the sea shack. After several steps, he turned and finally revealed what he had been getting at. "Andy, if you can't see how happy I have been since you came here, if you can't see how proud I have been of you this summer, if you can't see how much better my life is with you living here...then...oh, never mind!"

He continued his trek home to the sea shack. On the outside, his "never mind" was full of frustration, and you would think he had just given up on getting through to me. That wasn't it, though. Grampy just wasn't very big on talking about his emotions. Even as I grew older, it was rare for him to say how he felt about other people. The funny thing was, he never had to say it. You always just knew. He had a silent way of letting you know when he was happy with you, or when something was wrong. That night on the beach, though, he said just enough to make me think. I stayed on the beach a while longer, just thinking. Had I ever made anyone proud before? Did I really make his life better by being there? I wasn't used to this. I wasn't used to knowing I meant that much to someone. Even when my father had said "I love you," he said it so much and so quickly that it seemed to lose its meaning.

As cold as it was on the beach that night, something kept me warm. Once again, I had changed in a big way. As sad as it may sound, I truly believe that that was the first time I really felt like I was a very valuable person, that I was really important. With my antics at home and problems in school, I had become used to feeling like I was "in the way," or a "disruption to class," or any other sort of "problem." Now I felt like gold. I felt like I was the king and that my throne was suddenly full of treasure. I was *important*, and it felt great. Many people had told me I had the "gift of the gab," but, as I said, Grampy was the exact opposite. He could keep his mouth completely closed and still tell you what he was thinking or feeling. That evening, he never actually said the three words "I love you," but I felt more loved than I ever had before. I felt appreciated, and I felt like I was truly wanted. Knowing how my grandfather felt about me was extremely important, but so was the other lesson I'd learned that night. More than anything, I had learned that knowing people are proud of you and love you is far better than any other feeling in the entire world. That feeling had been missing in my life all along, and it made me wonder just how "perfect" life before Grampy really had been.

CHAPTER 14

After my grandfather had walked back to the sea shack, I felt as if I could have sat in the sand all night long. I don't know if it was all the thoughts that were stampeding through my head or all the feelings that were melting into my heart, but something froze my entire body that night and just left it sitting in the sand. I have no idea exactly how long I was out there, but I finally reached the point where I also returned to the sea shack. Was I done with all the thinking, or did it just get too cold? I think it was more the cold, because for most people it takes months, even years, to figure out all the things in their heart and mind: I had only just begun to work it out.

One of the other nice things about Grampy was that he always watched out for me without making me feel like a baby. When I walked in, he had gone to his room and was in his bed, but I knew he was not asleep. It felt good knowing he treated me like I was mature and responsible, but at the same time, it was nice to know he wouldn't sleep until I came in. He kept watch over me, but he didn't yell at me. He made sure I was safe, but he didn't lock me in the house. He did all the things he was supposed to do, but he let me be who I was and made me feel like I was at least a little grown up.

One other funny thing about major emotional events is all the energy they drain from your body. I didn't fight any fish that night, and I didn't do any real exercise, but when I got into bed I was completely exhausted. I fell fast asleep within a minute, I think. Morning was not far away, but I slept so deeply it felt like one of the best rests I'd ever had.

I didn't really need Grampy to wake me up anymore. I had adjusted to his schedule, and the sun's rays were enough to draw my eyes open in the morning. Not only was I adapting to Grampy's way of life, but I was almost starting to enjoy it. Some mornings I got up early and felt even better than when I slept in. I had to admit there was something nice about waking up with the sun and getting every bit of light out of the day.

As I bounded out the bedroom door, I must have been a mixed picture. I had a smile on my face because I was finally looking forward to the day ahead with Grampy, but I was still rubbing my eyes and scratching at my head a bit, showing hints of the boy who still enjoyed sleeping late. Grampy was just about done cooking breakfast on the stove—those bull's eye I loved so much—and he had also cooked up a batch of bacon, too.

"You're getting to be quite the morning bird, huh?" He looked at me with a smile as he placed my glass of orange juice on the table.

"Well, you're just going to wake me up anyway, so why stay in bed, right?" I felt like it was still my kid duty not to act too happy about the early mornings.

"Good point. You're smart to get up. Never know when your next cold shower will be."

As I thought back to that first morning when I'd been doused in the icy splash, I saw a smirk twitching at the corners of Grampy's mouth. I grinned at Grampy as I picked up his joke: "That's right. It's nice to stay dry. Plus, I'll have plenty of time to sleep when I'm gone, right? Nobody's going to throw water on me in Marshfield!"

I began to laugh out loud, realizing how funny the whole incident seemed to me. I turned to see my grandfather laughing, but he had stopped. He had become serious again, and a small bubble of concern grew in me. Had I said something wrong? Was it a bad idea to joke with him? Didn't he get it? I was only having fun! A few weeks back I would have been more worried, and that worry would have driven me into total silence, but now I spoke up. "What's wrong? What did I say?"

"Oh...ummm...nothing. Don't worry about it. You're right—no showers in Marshfield." I could tell something was bothering him, something I had said.

"Grampy, what did I say? I was just trying to joke around, okay? I guess I should be more serious."

"No, it wasn't that. I just don't think you know what it really means, that's all."

I paused, and I thought about his saying. What it really means? What it really means? It's a pretty simple phrase. How hard can it be? *You'll have plenty of time to sleep when you're gone.* I struggled to put the pieces together in my brain. When I go home, nobody makes me get up early, so I'll have all the time I want to sleep. Right? What was I missing?

Suddenly, it felt like an invisible boulder was dropped on my head. It hit me. It hit me hard, it hit me fast, and I got it. Being "gone" had nothing to do with Marshfield. Being "gone" meant being dead. It was a thought that absolutely terrified me. Of all the things in the universe, death was the one thing I could never bear to think about. My face must have gone pale when it dawned on me what he meant. I wasn't laughing now either; not even a trickle of a smile was left. "Does it mean death, Grampy? Being gone?" Part of me almost hoped he wouldn't answer.

"Yes, it does, Andy. It means that you sleep a long time after you die, so you better take the time to enjoy life now."

I couldn't find the words. Nothing came out of my mouth. I just sank really low, sliding down in my chair. How completely depressing. There were many things my grandfather taught me that summer, and many things I was still hoping he would teach me, but death was something I did not want to know about. It shook me down to my bones. The worst was when I'd be in bed at night, thinking about it, and then I couldn't fall asleep because the idea made me feel so sick.

"What's wrong, Andy?" he said, as if he had no idea why I'd become so quiet—as if he had no problem at all with the idea of death.

"I hate death. I hate thinking about it. Why would you tell me that saying, anyway? Why did you teach me a saying about death?"

He sighed heavily, just as I had seen him do so many times before. "Listen, Andy. It's not a message about death: it's a message about life."

"It's about life?"

"Yeah." We were back to the short and simple answers, the ones that made me think things over on my own. I couldn't figure it out, though. I said it over and over and over to myself, and every single time that one word was louder than all the others: gone. I knew what gone meant now, and I wished I had never found out. I had thought it was a neat little saying and had said it to myself so many mornings all summer long, and now I hated it. I hated that it was stuck in my head, and I hated that I had learned it so well. My dad had always told me never to use the word "hate," that it was too strong and terrible for people to use, but this was one thing that I thought I could use it for. The idea of dying disturbed me so much, made me so upset, and was so hard to get rid of that I honestly hated it. I wanted so badly to shake that feeling, to get my brain off that word "gone," but I couldn't. It would have been great if

Grampy had ended my silence with a better explanation, but instead he simply finished his breakfast and went about the chores.

"You going to get that flag up?" he said, as if everything was just as it had always been before.

I had totally forgotten about the flag and got right to work. Maybe doing some chores would help shake my troubles. I walked into his room and then carried the flag outside. As I unfolded it, clipped it to the pole, and slowly began to raise the banner towards the sky, my thoughts drifted to Grampy and his time in the war.

It seemed to be working. Raising the flag seemed to take my mind off death, until I thought about the soldiers who had died in the war, and then it came rushing back. *Gone, gone, gone.* It rang through my entire system like a loud, haunting bell that would not stop ringing, causing what felt like actual pain. Then, just when my agony over that word reached its peak, something truly spectacular happened.

It honestly was spectacular but, in a way, so unbelievably simple. I had just hoisted the flag to its highest point, and I looked up. The sight struck me with a sudden impact. That star spangled banner waving in front of the blue sky and white clouds was so amazingly beautiful. I had seen flags so many times, probably thousands of times, but I'd never really noticed the beauty, the glory of the American flag unfurled against the background of a bright summer sky. My eyes began to scan the land around me, and my ears began to open to the sounds of this simple paradise. I looked over the biting grass and the waves of sand dunes. I watched the shore birds flying by in the morning light, and I heard them calling to each other as they danced in the wind. I tried to listen to each little sound they made. I listened to the sound of the waves rolling along the shore. It took me back to my lesson about how beautiful nature is, and that, at last, helped me understand. I realized at that moment just how awesome being alive was. Grampy was right; the saying wasn't about death; it truly was about life. How many people go through life without ever thinking how incredible it is to see a beach, to hear a bird calling, or just to breathe in cool morning air? Back home and in school, I had never even thought about these things, but somehow it was beginning to make sense now.

I rushed back inside, and before I could say a word to Grampy, my glowing cheeks and wide eyes gave my secret away. He smiled. "You get it now, don't you?"

"Yeah, I do! It's so funny, because it really does sound like a saying about death, but it really says you need to live. It's like we have so many awesome things around us every day, and we are here to enjoy them as much as we can, not sleep it away. Right?"

He was laughing at me again—not because I was wrong but simply because I sounded funny to him. As a kid, I used words and said things in ways he wouldn't even think of. I appreciated the laugh because I felt like our differences actually helped us grow closer that summer. He carefully composed himself, looked at me with his round red cheeks, and said, "Right."

CHAPTER 15

It was August now, actually a full week into August, and I knew my time with Grampy was going to end soon. It didn't bother me much at that moment, though. By that point in the summer, I had come to enjoy my stay so much that I didn't have time to think about leaving. It popped into my head every now and then, and I thought about home from time to time, but those moments always ended quickly once I started something new with Grampy. I think another reason why I didn't think too much about going home was my painting job. I was doing many new things, but I was still spending some time each day painting (unless it was raining too much). Even though I had slowed down a bit, I had plenty of time to finish the work. Grampy told me what a great job I was doing and he didn't seem to mind my slow pace. As long as I was doing the job right, not complaining too much about the work, and using the rest of my time to do other productive tasks, Grampy stayed fairly satisfied.

Through everything, though, there was one thing I still wanted to learn about, but I was afraid to bring it up. My lessons about nature were very special to me. Learning to cook and take care of myself were skills that I knew I would never stop using. Even back then, I understood that Grampy's lessons would always be important to me. Picking up all his little sayings and phrases was fun and educational in a different sort of way. By this time, I felt as if I could ask my grandfather to teach me about anything, and he would do it. The man I was once afraid of, the man whom I'd been so frustrated with, and so annoyed by, was quickly becoming more than a terrific grandfather: he was becoming a good and trusted friend. We had grown very close, and even though I believed I could ask him about anything, one topic stayed deep inside of me: the topic of my mother.

It had bothered me off and on ever since he had said I reminded him of her. I understood that I might look like her a little, and I could believe that I might talk and walk like her. I was even willing to believe I acted like her, and maybe made the same mistakes she had made when she was a kid. All of these things made me feel better about her. As I said before, I had never really given her too much thought until that summer, and thinking about her was definitely nice. But it just wasn't enough. Grampy had only told me a few things about her, and those things were like the first few potato chips out of a bag. Whenever I ate potato chips, I only needed to eat two or three, and then I wanted the whole bag. I'd get hooked. It was the same way with my mother. I had spent my whole life refusing to think about her, and after hearing just a few drops of information about who she was, I found myself craving more.

For whatever reason, though, I couldn't bring this up with Grampy. Believe me, there were many days and nights when I tried. I would look at him, open my mouth, and hear the words in my head, but nothing would come out. Was I afraid to ask? Maybe I just didn't know what to say. Perhaps I thought he wouldn't talk about it. After all, I knew that losing a daughter must be awfully painful. I did not know the reason. I only knew I could never bring it up. Instead, I found myself visiting his room more often. Anytime he was out of the sea shack, anytime I knew I was alone for a bit, I found myself in his room looking at pictures of her. He was right: she did look like me. Obviously, we weren't like twins, but I could almost see myself, especially when I covered her hair with my fingers.

There was one picture in particular that captured me every time I went in. It was a picture of her holding me in the hospital. It reminded me of that video I had buried in my closet back home. All those times I'd watched it, all those pictures I had looked at, and I had never really cared. I had never even taken a moment to think about them. Now I couldn't stop thinking about them. I stared at that picture, that image of her holding me in her arms and smiling from ear to ear. I saw how beautiful her smile was, and I even stood there in the room trying to smile the same way, wondering if my smile was just as perfect as hers. I looked at myself, too, so tiny and completely wrapped up in that blanket. Most of all, I wondered about things I might never know. What was she thinking in this picture? Was she saying anything to me? How long had she been holding me? There was an endless stream of questions and empty holes with no answers. It hurt me that I didn't have any answers, and it always took me back to my ultimate question: Why did she have to leave me?

I was very careful about looking at these pictures. I didn't want my grandfather to see me looking at them. Even with the questions rushing through my head, I would pause to look out the window and be sure he wasn't coming in. If I heard his footsteps, I would get out of the room as fast as I could, acting like I had never even set foot in there.

It was only a matter of time before I would get caught, though. I always tried to be alert enough that I could make my escape, but on this one day I was so wrapped up in that picture that I didn't notice anything else around me. I didn't notice how dark it had become outside the window. I didn't notice how hard it had started to rain or see the wild winds slashing past the shutters. I didn't hear footsteps coming through the front door, or hear Grampy come into the room and walk up behind me. I didn't notice anything until I felt his hand on my shoulder and heard a soft voice say. "You're thinking about her, aren't you?"

I was caught completely off guard. I put the picture back on his bureau where I'd found it, spun around to show off my embarrassed red face, and began to stammer, "I...I...I'm sorry. I was just...I...."

"Andy, relax. You should be thinking about her. She's your mother. It's normal for you to think about her, okay?" He took off his wet shoes, placed them in his closet, and put on the driest, warmest slippers he owned. Then he left me in there while he went out to make a cup of tea for himself. I didn't know what to think. I just sort of stood still in the room for a few moments, and then I picked the picture up again. He sat down with his tea as I walked into the kitchen, the picture still in my hands, my eyes still staring into it. I could feel the words coming now, rising up inside me. At the same time, I could feel the water building around my eyes. The first little tear rolled down just as the first words came from my mouth. "She really loved me, didn't she?"

I didn't cry much, just a few tears. They weren't even bad tears: in fact, I was relieved that I'd finally found the courage to ask about my mother. He gave me the same warm smile he had given me on the beach when he said he needed me, that special smile he saved for the moments when I needed it most. It was a smile that made me think that everything was going to be fine. He gave me that smile, along with the gift of these words: "Yes. She did. She still loves you, Andy."

I took a seat across from Grampy, still clutching the picture of my mother. "Still loves me? How? How can she love me if she is dead?"

"Bodies die, Andy, not souls." I had let those first few tears loose, and my eyes were dry now. I sat still and listened more carefully to him than I had ever listened to anyone else in my life. "Your mother's body stopped surviving, but her soul can never go away. She is still around you. She watches over you, she takes care of you, and she most certainly still loves you."

"How do you know?"

"How do I know? A few ways. First, she told me so. Shortly before she died, I had a long talk with her. I told her many things I wanted her to know, some things I had never told her before. She also told me many things. One thing she told me, something she wanted to make sure I knew, was that she'd always be watching over us both. She promised to take care of me, but she especially promised to take care of you."

I was in awe. The video at home was one thing, but actually hearing these stories of her seemed extra real to me. "How else do you know? You said there were a few ways. How else?"

"Well, I can still feel her. I can still hear her. It isn't easy to explain, Andy, but I can just feel her spirit still alive inside of me."

Long conversations with Grampy were very rare, and I had an idea how unique this was, to be sitting at the table with him discussing my mother. As I grew older, I would realize even more how special it was that he had taken so much time to talk with me that rainy afternoon. "Do...do you think she is inside me, too?"

"I don't know, Andy. Only you can answer that."

I took a long pause. My lips wrinkled up and I scrunched my face up a bit, as if I was physically trying to look inside myself. "I don't know." I wanted so badly to feel her, just like Grampy, but I didn't know what I was looking for, or even how to look for it. "What does it feel like?"

He laughed a little bit. Even I thought my question sounded kind of funny, but he did his best to give a serious answer. "It really is hard to tell you, Andy. Sometimes it is just a feeling of happiness: other times it feels warm. Sometimes it is even a sad feeling. It just feels like someone is there with you."

He went back to his tea while I continued to search inside myself. If she was with my grandfather, certainly she had to be with me, too. Right? Could she be with both of us? Maybe she just picked him over me. The harder I looked for her, the more I began to feel she wasn't there. During my conversation with Grampy, all the things he had said built up my hope. I'd grown more and more excited and eager to learn about her, but now I was becoming sad again. She wasn't there. I couldn't find her. My mother truly had left me.

I wished Grampy would give me an easy answer. That night would have gone much smoother if he just told me where my mother was so I could find her. That would have been great, but that didn't happen. Instead, the rain came down harder, joined now by some thunder and lightning. I wasn't myself that night, and I couldn't let go of that picture. I'd stare at her holding me, hoping to find that feeling that she was with me, whatever it felt like. Nothing came, nothing at all. It hurt to look so hard and find absolutely nothing. I didn't even want to stay up late that night. I dragged my feet towards my bed and lay down to go to sleep. I still couldn't let go of the picture, though. I placed it in *my* room now, on the bureau next to my bed, and Grampy didn't seem to mind. He pretty much left me alone that night, realizing, I guess, that I had a lot to think about. Lying there, I stared at the picture in the failing light, filled with disappointment. A few hours ago I had felt so much hope that I would learn more about my mother. But, I had learned nothing, and I felt nothing. I felt emptier than I'd ever dreamed possible. Eventually, I decided to give up, closing my eyes to get some sleep.

I listened to the rhythm of the rain on the window, the roll of the thunder, and the distant waves crashing into the beach. The one thing I liked about stormy nights was the way the sounds could make me relax and lull me to sleep. I let go of my worries as I listened to those sounds, and I felt my eyes getting heavier and heavier under their lids. I would be fast asleep within a few minutes—or so I thought.

"I love you."

My eyes shot open, wide as can be, and darted all around the room, searching for the person who had just said that.

"I love you," I heard it again, and again.

My eyes could have looked around the room all night and never have found a person saying anything. I soon realized that it had not been a person at all. The words were coming from that little voice I had always heard inside me, and that little voice was louder and clearer than ever now.

"I love you." That's what it was now saying to me over and over again. I listened more closely. "I love you." It was a gentle voice...a soft voice. It was the voice of a woman...the voice of my mother? Was that it? I listened again. "I love you." I sprang from my bed. That was it! She was with me, after all! Grampy had once told me that if you look for something too hard, you are bound to look right past it. That night, I spent every drop of energy I had trying to force myself to find my mother's spirit, and it was only when I completely gave up and let myself drift off to sleep that I realized she had been with me all along.

Grampy was still awake, watching the news on TV, when I ran out to the kitchen. "She *does* love me. I can hear her. You were right! She *is* still with me!"

He pushed a chair out from the table, inviting me to sit down. "I told you so," he said. "As long as you live, Andy, her spirit will always stay with you."

As wonderful as all the things were that Grampy had given me that summer, this moment was by far the most special. The moment when I realized my mother was still with me, that the best part of her had never left me, was another huge moment in my life. My father had never really said much about why she died so young and now, more than ever, I wanted to know as much as I could about her. All the questions I had never cared about seemed to need answers now. A more patient person would have gone back to bed right then, expecting only to learn more in time. I was never a patient boy, though, and, besides—I would have plenty of time to sleep when I was gone. For now, I wanted to know about my mother, and I finally felt comfortable enough to just come out and ask.

"Grampy? What happened to my mother? Why did she die?"

"I'll tell you what. It's late, it's rainy, it's cold, and we've both had a long day already. Let's get some sleep, and I'll tell you the whole story tomorrow."

As you must have figured out by now, "no" is a word you don't say to my grandfather too often, but this was a definite exception. I knew I would not be able to sleep and put this off until the morning. "No, Grampy. I want to know now. Please tell me?"

He waited a moment, and I could tell he was thinking it over. My grandfather stuck by his routine and was firm in his lifestyle, but he also knew some things were just too important. Telling the story that needed to be told meant staying up later than he or I normally did, but he knew it was important enough to break the routine. "Okay," he said, "I'll tell you what happened."

That was the night of August 10th. It was the night I learned what a remarkably strong and truly amazing woman my mother had been. That was the night that she became my hero.

CHAPTER 16

I knew that what my grandfather was about to tell me would be a long story because he made himself another cup of tea before he started, and he never had tea this late. He made his cup, brought it over to the table, and began to tell me all about my mother.

"I guess the best place to start is back when she found out she was pregnant. She had been going on and on for a while about how much she and your dad wanted to have a baby. They had been married for two years then, and I think they knew from day one that they wanted kids and a family. They just wanted to wait until they were ready: they wanted to make sure everything would be perfect. I can still remember the day she told your grandmother and me the good news. I was so happy for her, and looking forward to being a grandfather, but your grandmother was a sight to be seen. She couldn't stop hugging your mother and letting out happy little squeals and talking all the baby talk she felt she needed to say. As happy as your grandma was, though, nobody was as excited as your mother. She wanted a baby in the worst way, and we all knew it. Everyone was so happy for her when she found out you were on the way."

So far, I was enjoying the story. It was all good news to this point and I felt the warm glow of feeling wanted and loved as my grandfather described my mother's excitement.

Grampy sipped his tea and then continued with his story. "Anyway, things got crazy after that. Your folks were both wild about a baby coming. Your mom began doing everything right away: shopping for clothes and baby stuff, thinking of names, reading books, buying magazines, even looking at schools in the area so she'd know what was best for you. She put your dad to work, too. He spent almost all his free time setting up a new room in the house, a room just for you. I helped him fix some parts of the floor and put up wallpaper. He put in new lights, and a new carpet, and he even made a few things by hand that you could keep in the room. Your mother told me over and over that she wanted everything to be just right, that she wanted all the best things for you. Both of them wanted to be sure that you were treated like a king from the minute you arrived, and no job was too big or too small to do for their new baby."

When all you have ever known about your mom is that she got very sick and died, hearing stories from when she was healthy and happy changes a lot of things. When I tell this story now, some people think the parts about her shopping or visiting my grandparents are not very important to the story, but to me they were very important. This was really the first time I had heard any stories about her not being sick. These stories were about an energetic and joyful woman, a woman I know I would have loved. It was a new way of looking at her, and it was information that I needed to help me learn who she really was. Grampy was tired, and his pauses seemed pretty long, but I was able to push him along with my anxious eyes and fidgety motions.

"Okay. Like I said, your folks were both looking forward to you being born. If you'd searched the whole country, finding two people as excited as they were would have been a challenge. It really seemed like everything was going along just fine, until your mother went in for a doctor's appointment in November. She was almost four months pregnant with you at the time, but she had new questions for the doctor because of some problems that had come up. Just a couple weeks earlier, she had been over at our house talking about her back and how badly it had started to hurt. She described how painful it was on some days and how it seemed fine on other days. She also mentioned that she'd begun to have some strange feelings in her chest. They weren't really pains, but they were odd enough that she decided to ask the doctor about them. When she told me about those problems, I got a bad feeling. I don't know much about women at all, but I knew enough to think something wasn't normal. In any case, she went to the doctor, they did some tests, and then she got the worst news she could imagine: She had cancer."

My jaw dropped open. I knew what cancer was, but I had never known that my mom had had it. People had said she was very sick, but for whatever reason they had never told me what she actually got sick with. Even as a child, I had heard a lot about cancer and most of the stories were not good. I also did not know that my mother had gotten sick at the same time she was pregnant. I always just assumed that I was born and then she'd gotten sick after that.

Grampy let out a deep, heavy sigh and blinked his eyes a few times. He rubbed them as if he were tired, but I could tell he was a little sad telling the story. He did not cry, but his face told the whole story. It was hard for him, but he was telling me because he really believed I needed to know. "Cancer. It was the last thing your mom and dad expected to find. They were totally shocked. They didn't know what to do. Back then, they did not have the same medicines and machines we have today. It is still so hard for people to get rid of cancer, but it was even harder then. Your mom was lucky, though, because her cancer was actually discovered fairly early. I drove her and your father to the hospital a few days later. They had a long meeting with a doctor whose specialty was in treating cancer. He explained that there were many things they could do, and some gave her a decent chance of surviving, but there was no guarantee. No matter what they did, there was still a chance they wouldn't beat the cancer and she would die from it. He was very clear, though, that they had found hers early and if they started to treat her right away, she had a good chance to live. At first, this was great news. Your mom felt much better knowing she had a good chance to live. It was hard to deal with, being so excited about life with your new baby and then finding out you had cancer. To this day, I am amazed she was able to handle it as well as she did."

"So, did she get better? What did she do? The medicine didn't work, did it?" I was completely wrapped up in the story and could not stand even the shortest pauses. I kept prodding him to go on until the next words came out.

"Well, there was one more problem. You see, Andy, many of the things they do to treat cancer are designed to actually kill the cancer. The problem is that the treatments usually don't just kill the cancer: they kill other things in the body, too. Sometimes this means a person's hair falls out, or skin problems develop, or another organ develops its own problem. The doctors told your mother that any of those things could happen to her. But they also told her one more thing that would happen, something that she just couldn't bear: she wouldn't be able to have the baby. The treatment they were going to give her used certain medicines and something called radiation. Both of those would most likely severely hurt the baby or kill it. You need to know, Andy, that as much as cancer terrified your mother, the idea that she could lose you was even worse. She did not *have* to go through the treatment, though. They couldn't force her. She knew she had a choice. If she tried to kill the cancer inside her, she had a good chance to survive but her baby would not. If she refused to get treatment, she could have her baby, but that meant the cancer would grow larger and become much worse. She asked both your grandmother and me for our advice, but we knew it was a decision she had to make. As strong as I like to think I am, I don't know if I could have ever made that choice. It was a really hard time for everyone. What had seemed like a dream come true was falling apart, and it really looked like an impossible decision for her to make. Well, Andy, your mother...she always had a way of surprising me. It was the very next morning that she came over, looked me right in the eye, and said "Dad, I'm going to have this baby."

There was no pause this time, just a short breath, a hard swallow, and he kept going. "It was one of the few times in my life when I was truly speechless. I did not know what to think. On one hand, I was filled with sadness, fear, and probably a little anger, too. Looking at my only daughter, who was deciding to face death, was almost too much for me. I couldn't bear the thought of losing her. On the other hand, I was full of pride. She knew she would lose a good chance at surviving, and she decided that it didn't matter. Nothing was going to change her mind. She had decided that her child was more important than she herself. Now, if that isn't a loving mother, I don't know what is. She hadn't even seen your face yet, but she was ready to risk her life for you. For some people it is hard to understand that, but when you have your own children, you know why she did it. You know how much love you have for your children, and they really do become more important than yourself. It was odd, in a way, because I would have gladly taken the cancer myself if it would have meant saving my daughter...so I knew exactly how she felt about you.

"As proud as I was of her the day she told us her decision, I only became more proud of her during the months that followed. They did have some medicine that was safe for her to use, medicine that wouldn't hurt you and could possibly control the cancer a little. She took the medicine just as she was supposed to, but it didn't help much. Her tumors got larger, and they spread to other parts of her body. It was only a few more months until you were to be born, but cancer can spread like fire. More tumors also meant more pain, and things were getting very difficult for her. Every doctor's visit brought more bad news, except for the ones that told us how well you were growing and developing inside her. In spite of all the pain and discomfort she had, talking about her baby would always make her smile.

"Soon, you had grown enough to be born and you came into our world. Your mother began to go through treatment right after the birth, but it was too late. The cancer had done too much damage and there wasn't much the doctors could do. They tried their best, and on some visits it looked like things were getting better, but then they'd only go bad again. Every time our hopes rose, something would bring them down. The treatments couldn't save her life, but they gave her one precious thing: time. She had time to hold you, to love you, and to talk to you. I know you can't remember it, but she talked to you every day and sang to you every night. She knew she didn't have much time left to spend with you, and she wanted to enjoy every second she had. It was heartbreaking to watch, heartbreaking for her, too, of course, but it proved to everyone what a strong woman she was. She never wanted to stop holding you. As soon as she decided to let you go or put you down, she'd change her mind and want to hold you even longer. You were her greatest treasure and she loved you more than anything in the world.

"We talked a lot in the days before she finally passed away, and she told me many things. I remember she was holding you one night and had just finished singing a song to you. She looked at you sleeping in her arms and then she looked at me and whispered the most important thing of all: "He was worth it. He was definitely worth it."

"Everyone saw that, Andy. Everyone saw that you really were worth all the pain and trouble she had gone through. She had made a hard decision. She decided to give up her own life so that you could be born and be healthy. That's how much she loved you, Andy. That is how much you meant to her. People always say that it was a decision that cost her her life, but that is not the most important thing. The most important thing is that, yeah, she passed away, but right until the very end she knew that it was the best decision she had ever made."

CHAPTER 17

The night my grandfather told me all about my mother, and how she had given her life up for me was another sleepless night. It was another night spent with my eyes wide open in bed, staring at the ceiling in my room and listening to the rain. My mind and heart were fixated on death, but now it brought a new feeling with it. It wasn't as scary as it was before, and it didn't give me that same sick feeling. I wasn't looking at it as the end of anything. Instead, I tried to picture those people all around us, listening to us and watching us. I used what I had seen in the videos and photos to imagine my mother in the room there with me, watching over me as Grampy had said.

I wondered if she was still watching me right now. I wondered what she thought of all the things I had done, and if she really was watching me *all* the time. Obviously, there were some things I hoped she wasn't watching. At first, I flashed back to all the big moments in my life: goals I had scored, games I'd won, birthday parties, vacations, jokes, tricks, trips with dad, days with my friends, everything and anything, big and small. I smiled to think that she was with me all these times, but the smile melted away as I began to think of other things. I thought of words I had said to kids in school, to teachers, and to other adults. I thought of fights I'd gotten into over the smallest things. I thought of mean pranks I had played on other people, and how hard I'd laughed when I saw them hurt or embarrassed. I thought of nights when I had refused to do any home-work, days when I had failed tests and said I didn't care, and days I'd acted sick just to stay home and play video games. I remembered things I had taken from people, or at least cheated them out of, and all the lies I'd told everyone around me, only caring about myself. It was true that everything was about me and not anyone else. I hadn't really cared about my friends, my teachers, or even my relatives. I loved my dad but had told him many lies, and I hadn't even cared about my grandfa-ther for most of the summer. As I lay there in bed, going through all these thoughts and memories, one question burned a hole deep inside me: What did my mother think? What did she think when she saw me doing all these things? How did she feel when she saw how I had been acting? I really believed, and in a way I *knew*, that my mother really was watching me and staying with me. I never felt it or saw it until that night with Grampy, but since then I had felt her every day of my life. I knew she was real, and I had the horrible feeling I had let her down. The idea that she might be disappointed in me bothered me a great deal. It was odd, in a way: For quite a while, living people all around me had been disappointed in me and had even told me so to my face and it never changed a thing. But the night I thought my mother, who had died, might be disappointed in me was the very night I decided that making a change might be a good idea.

After hearing my mother's story, things were kind of weird around the sea shack. Grampy and I were both quieter than we had been. I knew that telling the story had been hard for him, and hearing it had given me a lot to deal with. We both needed a little time to get back into our normal routine. The quiet allowed me to spend more time on my painting and, by the end of the week, I had the job done.

Although Grampy had been talking to me much more in the last few weeks, he still kept to his "short and simple" style as much as he could. I longed to hear a speech, full of flowery praise, telling me that it was the best the old shack had looked in ages. But I knew that just wasn't my grandfather's style. He took a couple slow laps around the house, scanning and examining each section with an eye trained for scrutiny. A few times he rubbed his hand along the wood or peeked behind the shutters. He even knocked on the wood two or three times as if he expected all the paint to fall off. Finally, he gave me a quick slap on the back and simply said, "Good job."

He didn't need to say anything else. We were able to talk without words now. I knew what message every twitch of his eyebrow, wrinkle on his forehead, or curve of his lip was sending me, and he knew the same with me. Two words were more than enough. I knew he was happy with the job I had done, and proud that I had gotten it done in time. I had done my best, I hadn't taken any shortcuts, I'd never given up, and it was all worth it. Knowing that Grampy was proud of me wasn't the best reward: it was feeling proud of myself. Looking at those walls covered in fresh, gleaming white paint and knowing I had made it that way filled with me so much satisfaction. I had never really worked at anything before. I'd always run away from work or responsibility of any kind, and I had only done this because my grandfather had found some mystical way of pushing it on me. I was so glad he had, though. If not for him, I might have never learned what that "job-well-done" feeling was like. It was more than pride: it was a feeling of power and strength. Seeing the finished job, a job I once thought I could never do, made me believe I could do anything.

The strongest winds in the world could not have wiped the smile from my face that night. Even as darkness fell, I went out again to look at the new paint.

I was amazed at what I had done. I hard a hard time believing it was actually finished. Painting was such a part of every day that I didn't know what I would do with the time now that the job was done. I was sure Grampy would have other jobs for me to work on, but it would still feel a little empty without the painting. That was perfectly fine, though, because all I would have to do when I missed the paintbrush would be to look over and see how nice the sea shack looked now.

Suddenly, there was a knock on the door, something that rarely happened at the sea shack. I wondered if it was Mrs. Hewitt again. Only a few people had visited the sea shack all summer, and she was the only one I really liked. I didn't think this was another old person, though, since it was so dark. It was far too dark to walk along the beach, and Grampy's friends hardly ever drove at night. Nobody ever said it, but I think their eyes were going bad and they were afraid of crashing. One friend whom I met briefly, named Joe, was an extremely nice man but I had the hardest time not laughing at his glasses. They were the thickest glasses I had ever seen in my life, and so huge that they covered most of his face. As I listened, I knew for sure that this knock couldn't be from Joe, or any other old man. The sun had gone down for the day and I was almost nervous to find out who it was.

"Go get the door, Andy, will ya?"

"Me? You want me to get it?"

Even though I often had to ask him things *three* times, he expected to ask *me* only *once* and it would get done. The frustration was evident as he stared me down and repeated the request, with a much firmer and stricter tone now. "Yes! I want you to go and get the door. Okay?"

"Okay." I slowly stepped over to the door and pulled it open. Standing in the doorway was a man I was very familiar with. It was a man whom I had grown to love as a child, a man who brought some of the best gifts to our home in Marshfield. This was one of those people you wished would come to your door every night, all year long. He was one of those people who made you smile and almost start bouncing with joy the second you saw him. He was the Papa Gino's delivery-man, and he had a large, steaming, fresh, hot pizza in his arms!

Grampy paid for the pizza and placed it on the table with some paper plates. Then he let me get an ice cold Coke out of the fridge. He knew I loved Coke, but he usually didn't let me drink it with my dinner. I hadn't had pizza in so long that it was a sight for sore eyes. He had even ordered my favorite: sausage! Between bubbling bites of pizza, I joked with him: "You didn't feel like cooking tonight?"

He laughed. "No, I would have cooked, but every hard worker deserves a good paycheck. I know you've been waiting a while for this, so enjoy." He was right about that! I *had* been waiting a while for this. Since that morning after our big fight, when I'd first started to grow closer to him, he had taught me so many things about myself and other people. He had changed me in so many ways, but nothing could change my love for pizza. I savored every morsel of food that night and thanked him for the dinner. I also told him

200

something I guess he already knew: "You know what, Grampy? I really do feel good about getting that job done. Every time I go outside to look at it, it makes me feel proud all over again." He smiled. "Yep, I suppose that means you're starting to grow up, Andy." He also said that, "whether I liked it or not," I was starting to change and probably wouldn't be able to stop changing. In his "professional" opinion, I was a boy who was starting to mature.

CHAPTER 18

As happy as I was to have finished the painting job, there was one drawback to having reached that goal. With that job done, I quickly realized that I only had a little more time to stay at Grampy's. In fact, only a little over a week remained before my dad would come back. When I'd first come to Truro, my dad's return was a day I dreamed about. Back then, that last day at the sea shack had seemed so far away. Back then, I hadn't thought I could stand to wait to have my dad take me back to all my old friends. Now, a very big part of me wished I would never have to leave. I did miss my friends, and, by now, I missed my dad, too. I knew there would be some great things about going home, but I began to get an idea of how much I was going to miss my Grampy. He had become my wisest teacher, my best coach, and my most caring friend. The man who had been an old bore and a giant snooze in June had turned into a truly unique and special person. I didn't mind doing work for him anymore, I wasn't as angry as I had been before, and he somehow made me want to be a better person. He had become an important part of my life, a part I did not want to let go of.

I looked over at him as I threw my pizza-stained plate into the trash basket. "Grampy? You're going to come and visit us in Marshfield more, right? I mean, you have to."

"Yes, I'll visit more." He was watching the news now, dividing his attention between the TV and me.

"You have to promise, okay? You promise?"

"Yes, I promise. I'll visit. Don't worry about it." I could tell he wanted to watch his news program, and I sat down quietly, trying to watch it along with him. Some nights the news was interesting to watch, but most nights I tried not to pay much attention to it. I thought the news was important, but it was always something bad. This was my one big problem with the news: it was always all bad news. Well, almost all bad. I saw wars being fought all over the world, old people and young people being murdered, people losing their jobs and their homes, fires destroying buildings, honest people being ripped off by crooks, all sorts of people going to court with all sorts of other people, and all the other bad news you can imagine. I often sat there and looked at the TV, knowing there had to be good news to be found somewhere and wondering why they never put that on instead.

That night I made a big decision before going to bed. I swore to myself I would not argue with my grandfather over anything for the last week I was there. We were getting along really well, but just like all people, we still disagreed over small things here and there. We didn't have the big fights we used to have, but the little tiffs we all have with the people we love continued to pop up now and again. I wanted our last week to be perfect, though. I wanted it to be perfect for him so that we could save our best days for the last days. I wasn't sure when I would be with him again and I wanted to leave him with the best possible impression of me. I swore: no arguing, no fighting, and no complaining.

For the most part, I did a good job sticking to my promise. We had nice weather all week, and we stayed as busy as we could. We went fishing a few times, both during the day and at night. I caught two more striped bass that week and he was able to cut a lot of meat from the two of them. We put a few pounds of it into a bag and froze it so that my father could bring it home to Marshfield. We also made a plan to go and gather some fresh mussels early in the morning before he came to pick me up. I was going to surprise him with fresh fish and mussels. I was absolutely positive he would be stunned. Grampy was proud of me. I was proud of myself. And now I wanted my father to be proud also. I wanted him to know everything I had done while I was in Truro. Sure, it would be easy enough to tell him everything, but I wanted him to see it, feel it, and taste it, too. I wanted him to actually *know* the things I had learned.

We also spent a lot of our time walking and talking, strolling along the beach looking for odd things that the tide had washed in. It was only now, in the last week, that he stopped to ask me about school. He said how nice it would be to go back, and that is when I told him how hard school was for me and about all the troubles I had with teachers and other kids. The only thing he said to me was this: "I think you'll do much better this year. In fact, I'm quite sure of it."

There were very few things Grampy told me that turned out to be completely wrong, so hearing him say that made me feel at least a little better, but not entirely. "It's just so hard, Grampy. All the stuff we do is so boring and half of it doesn't make any sense."

"Well, you told me painting was boring, too, and look how that turned out. Just try it, Andy. Give it your best shot and see what happens. You know something? With all your complaining about work being boring and dull, you remind me of this man who was the fastest runner that ever lived."

"Really?" It should have dawned on me more quickly that my whining didn't really connect to running, but he hooked my interest. If I was anything like the world's fastest runner, that must certainly be a good thing.

"Oh yeah, this guy was built like a speed machine. Nobody on Earth was born to run like him. Not a single person was as fast or could run as far as he could."

"How fast was he? How far could he go?"

"Oh, nobody ever found out. Nobody ever heard of him. He never even became famous."

"What? Why not?"

"Because for his entire life, he was too afraid to put his running shoes on and try."

I thought it over for a minute and tried to make sense of it. It came to me slowly, but it did come to me. I wriggled my face in an annoyed way. "You just made that up, didn't you!"

"Maybe I did and maybe I didn't. The point is that you are never going to know how great you might be at something unless you sit down and try it. You are too busy complaining about your work. Just do your best and see where it takes you."

"If I do my best, will you come visit more?"

"I already told you I would visit more, didn't I?"

He had told me, but I needed to hear it again. I felt like the more I reminded him, the less likely he was to forget. I didn't want to lose him when the summer ended, and I would say it a million times if that was what it took.

"You need to stop fighting, too. I've watched you all summer and you're stronger than that."

Stronger than that? I had heard people give me all kinds of reasons not to fight: I was too smart, too mature, too responsible, and even too small—but too *strong*? That was a new one for me. "Too strong? What do you mean by that? How can you be too strong to fight someone? That is the whole point of fighting, isn't it?" My voice was full of confusion again.

"Strong people don't always have big muscles, Andy. The strongest people are strong from the in-side—like you. You said you get into fights if kids call you names or make fun of you, right?" I agreed with a nod. "Well, why don't you just walk away from them? Be better than they are and turn your back to them."

"I can't do that. They'd just keep doing it. It's too hard to—"

There it was. There was the answer. It was hard to walk away, and only a very strong person could do it.

"Kids like that want you to fight, Andy. They know you are going to fight them, and they say that stuff because they know it works. Every time you get into a fight, you are not standing up to them at all: you are just giving in to them. Standing up to them means walking away and refusing to let them win."

It took a little more thinking, but his theory did make sense. I couldn't begin to count the number of complicated things Grampy made simple and easy to understand that year. I always had to think a little to crack one of his riddles, but it almost always came down to one simple idea. So many times I was left asking "Why couldn't I figure that out?" and looking at him with even greater admiration. He was like a walking guide to life, a man who seemed to have it all figured out and who had let me in on his secrets. I promised to walk away from fighting, and, just for good measure, I gave him one more reminder of his promise to visit me more. I didn't care how old the promise got for him: it was important to me, and I needed to hear it.

CHAPTER 19

My dad came to pick me up on August 23rd. He arrived at the sea shack a little after Grampy and I had eaten lunch. I had talked to Dad on the phone a few times over the summer but I had never let him know how things were going—not since the first time we talked when I complained to him about everything. At the time, I was still angry about my summer being ruined, and my plan was to make him regret it as much as I could. But as time had passed, I had learned to love my grandfather. Just the same, I left all the good stories out of my conversations with Dad. I usually just told him things were fine and stayed quiet about all the details. I guess it was because I stayed so quiet about all those good changes that he was so surprised to see me smiling, running to hug him at first sight. I hadn't realized how much I'd truly missed him until I saw his truck pull up. It felt good to give him a big hug. I even told him I was sorry for the things I had said to him: "I really don't hate you, Dad. I was just mad: that's all. I didn't mean it."

"I know, Andy. Don't worry about it. We all say things we don't mean when we are upset." I don't think I could have done anything to upset him right then. A wide smile stretched out his face and made his cheeks glow under the lights. I knew he was happy to see me: the look reminded me of the one my mother had while holding me as a baby. It was that look parents get from time to time, when they are reminded how lucky they are to have children. That is one thing I have learned over the years. Parents absolutely love and adore their children, even those parents who get the most upset and have the most rules. Kids are the same way, actually. I had said many horrible things to my dad, and there were days I yelled as loudly as I could at him, but deep inside I never stopped loving him for a second, and I could never imagine having a different dad.

Grampy had stuck to our plan for that morning: we would treat my father to a welcome home dinner. He and I had gone out early and filled a bucket with fresh mussels. I skipped over to the fridge to show my father our bounty. When I told him *I* had gathered most of them, not Grampy, I knew he was a little shocked. I loved knowing he was surprised, and I knew how much fun it would be when I got to tell him about everything else I'd learned. I remembered the striped bass and ran back to the freezer to pull some of it out. "I hope you don't have plans for dinner already, Dad, because we were planning on cooking some fish and mussels for you tonight!"

"No, I didn't make any plans. Fish and mussels sound just fine." He was almost laughing, still a little confused as to how I was planning dinner for us. Then Grampy piped in, making the invitation for dinner at the sea shack official.

"I'll tell you what. Why don't you relax for a little bit. You don't need to rush home for anything right now, do you? Enjoy the beach and Andy and I will fix dinner for all of us. Good enough?"

My poor father looked perplexed. When he had left me at the sea shack, I was an angry and bitter child who had refused to show him a drop of love. That was all gone now, replaced by smiles and bubbling enthusiasm. I was happy that Grampy had offered to have dinner there because it meant the three of us would get to spend some time together. Dad sat down to unwind while we all talked about his trip. He described what it was like down in Texas and told us about some funny people he had met. He took a baseball out of his bag. He had gotten it signed by some players on the Texas Rangers and had brought it home for me to keep in my room. He took out some pictures that he'd already had developed, and Grampy and I were both full of questions as we browsed through them. As I listened to his tales about Texas, the same idea kept running through my head: Wait until he hears about *my* summer.

Dinner would be my chance to talk, my chance to tell him about all the things I had gone through with Grampy. It would also be time well spent with Grampy before I left. He and I talked while we cleaned off the mussels and prepared the fish. He gave me some final tips on how to cook them. He kept telling my dad he should go down to the beach to enjoy it, but Dad was too busy watching me. As I busied myself with the cooking and preparing the table, my dad's eyes shot rays of pride right through me. Of course he had been proud of me before, but this was different. He wasn't watching me in a game or a school play. He wasn't listening to something he had heard me practicing for weeks. This was something he did not expect at all, and the element of surprise made it all the better for him. I kept smiling to myself: I knew he'd never dreamed he would see me preparing the kitchen and cooking the food. I also knew he liked what he was seeing. I was not looking forward to going home in a few hours, but it was easier to deal with since I knew my father was enjoying himself so much.

Over dinner, I may have stopped talking only once or twice. I wanted Grampy to hear me talk about the things we had done, even though he turned a little red whenever I mentioned his lessons. I didn't know if they were supposed to be between him and me, but I really didn't care. It felt good talking about it all, hearing myself tell each story one by one. Sometimes you don't really know or understand something until you actually hear yourself saying it. Of course, by then I knew how special Grampy was to me and I certainly knew he had taught me a great deal that summer, but as I went through each tale of my education, even I was amazed by it all. Each little lesson or moment had become a precious memory for me, but when I put them all together, I understood better what a truly awesome experience my summer with Grampy had been. My lips were telling my dad about everything that had happened, but inside my brain I was talking to myself. I was telling myself how strange it was that an old man I swore I'd never understand had come to mean so much to me. I felt a flood of thoughts, emotions, and questions pulsing in my heart. I saw how proud my father was and imagined how proud my mother would have been. I wondered when I would get to come back to the sea shack and whether or not I would have to paint it again. I wondered when I would get to catch and cook my own dinner again. And, finally, I realized how happy I was at that moment. I was the happiest I had ever been—and I knew it was a feeling I wanted to hang on to. My life seemed much better now than it had been back in June. It was definitely a good thing, a feeling I savored, and I promised to keep that feeling as long as I could.

I wanted to talk all night long, but all things eventually come to an end. Dinner was long over, the dishes had been put away, my stories had begun to run out, and everyone was plenty tired. My dad slowly got up, stretched out his arms, and said it was time to go. For a moment, I think time stood still. I had known this was coming, of course. But even though I had been expecting it, when the time came to leave, it was still a shock. For a moment, I wished that I could stay and live there with my grandfather. Perhaps for a moment, I thought that I was just dreaming, that I would wake up any second and see it was still June. It was no dream, though. It was very real, and it was time for me to go home. I turned towards Grampy and tried to look up at him. It was hard to lift my head because my eyes were welling. They felt like they weighed twenty pounds each. I didn't have the words.

"Chin up," he said, "I'll come see you soon. Anyway, you need to go home and get ready for school now. Big year this year, right?" I could tell he was sad, too, even though he did a much better job of keeping it in.

"I'll miss you, Grampy." I stepped up close to him and wrapped my arms tightly around his waist, my head pressed against his belly. It was no ordinary hug. It was one of those hugs you give somebody when your soul is telling you not to let go. "You'll be okay, right?" I squeaked out. I knew it was a silly question to ask him, seeing as how he was the one who had taught me everything, but it was all I could think of to say. It matched what I was feeling inside.

"Of course I will, Andy. Don't worry about me. Get going now, move along." He shuffled me along out the door and toward my dad's truck. He still wasn't a man who liked to show too much emotion, and I think he wanted me on the road before too much began to leak out of him. I put the last of my things in the back of the truck and climbed into my seat. I couldn't take my eyes off Grampy. After I closed the door, he and my father said a few more things to each other in front of the headlights. I kept watching, almost hoping he'd turn and tell me I could stay. There was a handshake between the two men and then they parted ways. My dad made his way to the truck, into his seat, and fastened his safety belt. Grampy turned in the opposite direction and lumbered back into his shack.

Just as my dad pulled out of the driveway, I shouted out. "Wait! Wait!" I shouted so loud that Dad slammed on the brakes in a panic, asking what was wrong. "I just forgot to tell Grampy something. It's something really important, Dad. Okay? It will just take a minute." I wasn't sure if he would let me out of the truck again, so I gave him the saddest puppy dog eyes I could muster.

"Go ahead." He shifted the car into park and put his arm down on the seat. "I'll wait here."

"Okay!" I opened the door, hopped out, and rushed towards the sea shack door. Something had come into my head, and I was ashamed that I had not already said it to Grampy before leaving. I reached the door, pulled it open, and stepped back inside. He was sitting at the table with his tea. He looked like he was sad for a moment when I plopped myself in front of him, but then one of his warm smiles crept across his face. For a few seconds, we just looked at each other. No words were needed. Our eyes and our smiles said the same thing, that we were both happy for the time we had had together. Then I told him what I was so determined to make sure I said: "Thank you, Grampy."

Somehow, his smile grew even larger. He nodded his head, let out some kind of soft, warm sigh, and then he simply turned away to finish his tea. As I walked back out toward the truck, I turned for one last look. Through the window, I could see him lift his tea to his lips, and I smiled. I knew he was already slipping back into the reliable routine of his life. I thought to myself what a wonderfully simple man he was—and what a wonderfully amazing one.

That little "thank you" must have been powerful in its own special way. It made a huge difference in the trip home. I had expected that I would cry and mope all the way home. The sadness was incredible, more than I had ever honestly felt before, and I was certain I would be crying soon. Even when I first got into the truck, I could feel the tears ready to charge down my cheek. It was only after that "thank you" that the tears went into hiding and the smile came out to stay. I actually felt good on the ride home, and I wasn't sure why. Was it being with my dad again that made me smile? Was it knowing that my mom was with me? Was it going to see my friends again? (I *knew* going back to school wasn't bringing it on!) To be honest, I never figured out exactly what it was, but I know that saying "thank you" had a lot to do with it. Somehow, that was the most perfect and simple way to end my summer with Grampy.

CHAPTER 20

The days leading up to the start of school were a complete frenzy. I had so much to do and so little time to do it in. I needed new clothes, new supplies, and for sure, a new haircut. I had to catch up with all my friends and let them get caught up with me. I had to tell my dad all the other stories that popped into my mind, sharing each and every detail as if it were the most important thing I had said yet. Even adjusting to my house and my room took some time. I had gotten used to the cramped quarters of the sea shack, and now, back at home, our regular house felt like a palace. I had never thought of it as a big house until I spent the summer with Grampy. It made me wonder: *Why was the house so big?* Grampy and I were so happy in the sea shack, and it was all the space we needed. Suddenly, my house in Marshfield seemed almost too big for just my dad and me.

In the middle of this hurricane of activity, however, there was one person, more than anyone else near me, whom I felt I needed to get caught up with. I wasn't sure how I was going to do it, but I kept telling myself I needed to talk to my mom. There were things I needed to say to her, but it had to be the right place and the right time. Some people say you can't talk to people who have died, but I know you can. You don't even need to move your lips for them to hear you, even though some people do. Not only can you talk to them, but if you close your eyes and focus really hard, you can even hear them talking to you.

It was just about five days before school began when I finally asked my dad if I could visit my mother. I was afraid to ask for a couple reasons. For one thing, he had never taken me to her grave before, and I just assumed there was a reason for that. I figured that his keeping me away was his way of protecting me from something. I worried, too, that he'd think I was crazy. We had never gone to anybody's grave so I wasn't sure if it was normal or not. I'd heard, though, that many people go and visit loved ones at their graves, and I desperately wanted to visit my mother. I was simply afraid that if I asked to go see Mom, he'd think I had lost all my marbles or he'd begin to worry about me. On this particular afternoon, however, while he was preparing dinner, I mustered up the courage to ask. "Dad? How come you have never taken me to see Mom's grave?"

A pale shade covered his face, and he became very serious. Slowly he shut off the water that was running in the sink and sat down in a chair. The wrinkles on his forehead told me he was either thinking very hard, or that he was very confused.

"I...ummm...I don't know, Andy. I guess I should have. I just....well...."

"That's okay. I'm not mad or anything," I assured him. After spending time at the sea shack, I knew the spot he was in. I knew how hard it was when you felt like you should have an answer but simply couldn't find one anywhere. "Really, it's okay. I'd just....I'd just like to go see her before school starts...if it's okay."

He lifted his head, his lips pressed tightly together, and he seemed lost in thought. "Okay," he said. "We'll go tomorrow. It will probably be good to go see her anyway."

There was no more mention of the visit for the rest of that night. Through dinner, all through the ice cream we ate, and through the entire time we watched TV together, it did not come up again. The deal was made. We would be going to see her tomorrow. There just didn't seem to be much more to talk about beyond that. For a moment I was filled with pride that I had asked to visit her, but that pride soon became overshadowed by some fear. I had never been to a person's grave before. What would it be like? What would I say? How would I feel? There were too many questions even to try to answer, and I just did my best to stay calm. I just told myself to relax and let the answers come when they would.

Since I was still on Grampy's schedule, I was actually the one to wake my dad up the next morning. After some breakfast, he told me to go and start getting ready. In any other summer, this early start would have thrown off my entire day. It would have set me in a mood, and I would have carried that mood until bedtime. I was now a proud graduate of life with Grampy, however, and the early morning had little effect on me. It even took me back to the mornings in Truro when the cool morning breeze would tickle my face and the seagulls would all cry out their greetings. I quickly took a shower, got dressed, and went downstairs. I was still nervous and a bit worried, but I was also growing a little excited with each moment. Soon, my father and I were ready to leave. For this trip, we took the car instead of the truck. I was told my mother was never a big fan of trucks.

Along the way, my dad must have told me how nice I looked at least ten times. He had taught me to wear my nicest clothes when I went to church with him, and this almost seemed like the same thing. Whatever my reasons were, I had worn my fanciest clothes and I knew it had made an impression on my dad. We also stopped to pick up some plants along the way. My father bought a small green plant for Mom's grave and some flowers for me to bring.

"Your mother loved flowers," he told me, "She always smiled and looked perfectly happy when she was around flowers. Even if they were just by the side of the road, she'd take time to look at them or smell their fragrance." As he spoke, something was becoming more and more clear to me. I had asked to go visit my mother's grave because it was something I felt I should do. What I could see now, however, was that it would also be good for my dad. He had seemed reluctant at first, almost uncertain whether we should go or not, but as he was telling me about her love for flowers, along with other morsels of information, he seemed to be enjoying his own memories, almost as if he had forgotten how much they meant. We were getting closer to the cemetery where she was buried, and my nerves began to settle down.

The cemetery was enormous. As we drove along the road, I looked at all the headstones and all the names on them. Some were massive structures made of the smoothest stone you could imagine—more like statues than graves. Others were very small, just the size of a plate placed on the ground. There were those that were very new, including two where the ground looked like it had just been dug up recently, and there were those that looked ancient. I wondered what my mother's would look like. Was it one of the biggest in the whole cemetery, or did she have a little one? Was it one of the light-colored stones or dark? I even wondered about the people buried near her, as if they were next-door neighbors or something. Suddenly, Dad slowed the car to a stop, and he stepped outside. I turned my face to the right, and then I saw it:

Andrea O'Brien

Loving Wife, Mother, and Daughter

1961-1992

I felt a powerful force inside me the second I saw her grave. At once, I turned away and refused to look at it again. I wasn't afraid of it; I wasn't upset by it; but I couldn't make myself look at it. It just seemed very unreal to me, and seeing it for the first time overwhelmed me. I stayed close by the car with my head turned while my dad walked over to the grave. He knelt down on the ground with his face down and put his plant against the stone. He was completely silent for about five full minutes. I kept peeking over to be sure he was still there, but I still couldn't look at the words. After he got up, he slowly came over to me, wiping a tear from his cheek.

"I can bring your flowers over if you want, Andy."

"No, I'll do it...just...wait a minute."

"Okay, no problem. Take all the time you need."

I'm sure it was only a few seconds that I continued to stand by the car, but I carried on an entire conversation in my head during that time. I told myself I couldn't go over there, that I couldn't even look at her gravestone. Then I told myself that I had to, that I hadn't come all this way to back down. Then I knew I couldn't go, and then I was sure that I could. The debate raged on until I finally felt my feet begin to move.

Slowly, I trudged over to where she was resting. I looked back, almost hoping my dad was following me, but he was back at the car. He gave me a nod and a look, as if telling me to keep going, but he was letting me do this on my own. I made it all the way to her stone without looking up. I knelt down, and as I placed my flowers in the ground, a tear trickled down my cheek. I lifted my head and saw her name right in front of my eyes, and then the tears began to flow as if from a well deep inside my heart. I didn't have a chance of stopping them. I began to cry more than I ever had before. I didn't even care if someone saw me there, sobbing and kneeling in the grass. I felt incredibly guilty. I felt pure shame for never having gone to visit her before. My heart felt like it was crumbling to pieces as that guilt and shame tore away at me. Everything continued to build up until it began flowing out of me in words, soft quiet words for my mother.

"I am so, so sorry, Mom. I know I should have come to see you a lot sooner. I'm sorry. I just...I just didn't know what to say...or what to do, I guess. It isn't that I didn't think about you. I *did* think about you: I just, well. I don't know what to say, Mom. I wish I had the words, but I don't. All this time I thought you'd left me, that you were just gone and were never there for me. I feel so bad that I'm only coming to see you now. I just hope you're not too mad at me. Listen, I made a bunch of mistakes. I should have been talking to you a lot more, and I wasn't. I promise I am going to do better, though. I swear. I don't know—maybe you are the one who made me spend the summer with Grampy. Maybe in heaven they gave you special powers so you can make things like that happen. Were you mad at me for not coming to see you? I really hope not. I love you so much, Mom. Grampy told me all about you. He told me how you could have gotten the medicine you needed, but you didn't want me to be hurt. He told me that you risked losing your life so I could be a healthy baby. He told me how much you used to hold me and sing to me, and how you always talked to me. You're still talking to me, aren't you? That little voice I hear. I know it is you. It took me a long time to figure it out, but I know it is you. I know you are with me, Mom. I want you to know how much I really do love you and how much better I am going to do now. I will make sure I come visit you whenever I can, and I'll be sure Dad comes, too. He doesn't say it a ton, at least not to me, but he really misses you. Grampy misses you, too. We all miss you, and we all love you. I wish you had been around more as a living person, but I am glad you were always there as a spirit or ghost or whatever. I think you have been with me my whole life, helping me out when I was in trouble and trying to show me the right way. I didn't listen all the time, but now I know it was you. I will listen more, too, I swear. No more trouble for me. I really want to do better with schoolwork and stuff. I don't know if you can help me get better grades, but if you can, I hope you do. I want to do it, but I think I am going to need a lot of help. I don't know what else to say, Mom. I don't know if there is anything else you want me to say. I guess I'll just make sure I tell you the most important things before I go. I want to be sure you know how much I love you and how much you mean to me. Maybe it is bad that Grampy had to help me see that, but I do see it now and hope you can feel how much I love you. Also, thank you. Thank you for giving me so much attention when I was a baby, and thank you for risking your life for me. I used to get jealous when my friends got cool gifts from their moms, wishing you were here to give me things. Now I know that you gave me the best gift ever. I know how hard that must have been, and I will never stop thanking you for taking such good care of me. I miss you, Mom, and I love you. I hope you are proud of me, but I am not sure if you are. I've been in a lot of trouble and done some stupid things. I do swear that I will do better, though. I'll do everything I can to make you proud of me and, like I said, if you can help me out at all, I might just need it. Thank you, Mom. Thank you for everything you did. I love you."

After I was done talking, I thought about her for a few more minutes. I reflected on everything I had learned, and I felt a lot better. Tears continued to run down my face, but they weren't so bad now. Inside, it felt like I had made my peace with Mom and that I could move forward now. Until that day I had felt as if

I was a disappointment to her. She'd given up her life for me. Had I been good enough for her? No. That was how I felt, anyway, but talking to her changed that. It is like I said before, how dead people can talk to you without words. I heard no voices that day, but I felt much better when I left, as if she had said, "It's okay. I love you, too, and I am very, very proud of you." I could hear her and feel her all through me. Not all words are spoken: some come straight from the heart.

The talking was done and, although I had a difficult time walking away from the grave, I knew it was time to leave. I dried up as many tears as I could, ended my pacing around the stone, and went back to my father. He shared a long hug with me and then we headed back home.

More tears came on the way home, and then even more when I decided to watch my video of her that night. I watched that video of her holding me and talking to me with a whole new set of eyes now. It took on so much more meaning, and I felt so many more emotions this time. The video I had thought so little about a few months ago was now a valued gift within my heart. I cried as I watched it and even saw a tear or two on my dad's face. All I could think as I watched this treasure unfold was how brave my mother had been. It still amazed me that she had risked her own life for mine. I listened again to the way she talked to me in her soft, loving voice, and I said a silent thank you that she had given me this gift. As long as I had this video, I could visit my mother anytime I wished. Every minute or so I would wipe at my cheek, hoping to stay as dry as I could. It was a weak effort, though, and even my clothes began to moisten from the heavy drops. Through the tears, however, my smile never left me. These were not tears of sadness in any way. These were tears of joy, the type of tears most people don't mind too much.

CHAPTER 21

Just like every September, the first day of school came rushing upon me. It was a weird feeling, in a way, being around so many kids and adults. It reminded me just how much I really had adjusted to life with Grampy. We had never been around many crowds or large groups of people. He certainly wasn't one to make a lot of noise, and we hardly ever had visitors at the sea shack. Now, I was spending my day in classrooms of at least twenty other students, listening to other people the whole time and dodging traffic in the halls. A year ago this would have seemed normal, not a big deal at all, but now it seemed like chaos. For those first few weeks I came home from school each day exhausted, not from painting or fishing like those times with Grampy, but simply exhausted from being with so many people all day!

I got used to it again after just a few short weeks, but I can't say things ever went back to *normal*. That doesn't mean that life at school became *abnormal* after that summer; it just means that a lot of things changed for me. For starters, I began to listen more in class, and I actually pushed myself to get the best grades I could. There had been so many times when I'd said I was trying my best, maybe even *thought* I was trying my best, but I really wasn't. That year, I began to find out what my best really was. I'd love to say I earned straight *A's* and blew away all the other students, but that simply isn't true. What I can say is that I got better grades than I ever had before—nothing lower than a *B*. I didn't need to be the *very* best, just *my* best. Before that summer with Grampy, I had never realized that I should give my best effort to everything I did, including schoolwork. I had thought it was important to try to be the most popular and the funniest kid in class. I also thought I needed to be the strongest whenever I could be. Some days I thought I needed to be the fastest, and some days the loudest. I had tried to be many things, but never "my best." When that new school year began, one thing was clear: It was time for me to be the best I could be.

I started out by trying to be a nicer person. For a long time, I had picked on a boy named Kyle who stood out in our grade. Kyle was the one my friends and I had called "nerd," "loser," "idiot," and several other cruel names. He was a shy, small kid who wore thick glasses. He was an easy target. In the past, I'd pick on him and the others would laugh. They'd tell me how funny I was for doing all sorts of cruel things to him. It made me feel popular. It was different this year, though. Picking on Kyle made *me* feel like the loser, and I even got angry when I saw my friends doing it. It wasn't funny anymore, and I finally stood up for Kyle. I did my best to be his friend, but it took a long time. I had hurt him in the past, and it would be a while before he would trust me. That was new for me. Sticking up for kids like Kyle was something I had never tried before. As nice as feeling popular had been, simply doing the right thing blew it out of the water. I still felt popular with my peers, but now it felt even better. I began to learn the feeling of pride one gets from helping others. I was learning how awesome being my best really was.

Things began to change at home, too. From the minute he picked me up in Truro, the feelings between my dad and me seemed different. He was acting the same as he always had, and I don't think I was doing anything much different. On the surface, we appeared to be the same two people we always had been. Inside, however, it was as if our hearts were under construction, getting stronger and larger than they'd ever been before. After sharing my stories from Truro with him, he began taking me out fishing and swimming at the beach more. He even took me to Martha's Vineyard one day. We rented a fishing boat in the morning and rode bikes around the island all afternoon. We made more frequent trips into the city, and we played more games together at home. We planned a garden of our own for the yard and I sold him on hanging a flag by our front door. So many different things were important to me now, and Dad understood that. He understood how much I had changed, and I think he enjoyed the ways we were growing closer together.

Best of all, we talked about Mom more than we ever had before. He told me stories on a regular basis and each one helped me get to know her more and more. Not only did I get to know her better, but I also learned more about myself and where I had come from. I was amazed how much of her life reminded me of my own. Dad and I even made an agreement to visit her and talk to her more often.

I might never have gotten to know my mother if I hadn't spent that summer with Grampy. I think bringing Mom back into our lives helped my father, too. I knew he was grateful that I had asked to see Mom's grave and that I looked for more stories about her. He knew her so well and loved her so much, but he had locked all his memories of her away in a dark closet while raising me. He had stopped talking about her, talking to her, and had stopped spending any sort of time with her at all. It wasn't that he'd stopped caring; he just had not known what to do. He couldn't decide if he should raise me while telling me all about her or just raise me and let me learn on my own, so he just had to do what he thought was right.

Perhaps Dad had forgotten how nice it was to feel close to her, because each time we talked about her or went to see her grave, he wore an expression like no other. It was the expression of someone who is catching up with their old best friend; a friend they had not forgotten but had neglected for far too long.

Things continued to get better every day. School became a much nicer place for me, filled with new friends whom I enjoyed even more than the old ones. I felt happier with myself as a person than I had in a very long time. Most important, I felt as if I was a part of a family again. I felt closer to my dad than ever before, I could hardly stop telling people about my grandfather, and I couldn't stop thinking about my mother for a second. She was always with me. That little voice that had followed me through school all along had an identity now, a very special identity.

I could see the change in me and everyone around me could see it, too. It pleased me to hear people say that I was a "whole different person". I understood what they meant, but the idea was silly to me. I hadn't actually become someone new. People don't change: they just learn more about themselves and find who they truly are. Over time, people grow a little and listen a lot, and they begin to see the person they are inside. That's all I was doing. I was simply discovering how good I could really be.

For a while, I gave credit to Grampy for all these changes. I told myself, and everyone around me, that he was the one who had changed everything. It seemed obvious to me that I was going through all this change for him, to make him proud of me. The more I thought about it, though, the more uncertain I became. Was I really doing the best I could just to please Grampy? Maybe not. Sure, I wanted him to be proud, but perhaps that wasn't what drove me to work harder and aim higher. Was I doing it for my dad? I didn't think so. What about my mom? That answer made sense to me. It seemed logical that I wanted my mom to be happy with who I was so I'd work to do better for her. Time would show, however, that she was not the main reason, either. The person I wanted to turn things around for the most was my own self. Doing good deeds felt incredible, bringing home high grades made me feel proud, and spending time outdoors with my father made me feel as if I was actually a part of him. He continued to buy me nice gifts, but they just did not mean as much now. The best gift my father ever gave me as a child was the gift of his time. I kept asking myself, though, especially when things seemed to become difficult, "Who am I doing all this for? Who am I trying to impress?" I needed to spend a long time thinking this question over, but finally I realized I was doing it all for me, myself. I had tasted the excitement that came with doing well and now I craved it. I wanted to make others happy, and I wanted to go "above and beyond".

As I said before, things did not really go back to *normal* after that summer, but the change was a remarkable shift for me. Sometimes, going back to *normal* isn't a good thing. One of my teachers once said, "How would you ever know the warmth of the sun if you were always too afraid to go outside?" That, in a way, sums up what happened to me. I had been afraid of so many things; afraid of trying harder at school, afraid to walk away from bad situations, afraid to be totally honest with anyone else around me, afraid even to talk about the mother I had never known. I was no longer afraid and Grampy was the man who had helped me overcome those fears. He was the one who gave me the bravery I needed to face them. I was turning things around for myself, but Grampy was the man who showed me how it was done. Because of his believing in me, I was able to learn everything about myself. I finally knew who I was, and that incredible feeling radiated through my body like the rays of a bright, warm sun.

CHAPTER 22

I can still tell you what day it was. It was Thursday, December 15th. I was working on an assignment in my history class when the secretary from the office came in to talk to my teacher, Mrs. Johnson. I got a wrenching feeling in my gut. Somehow I knew it wasn't good. Mrs. Johnson waved her hand, signaling me to come up, and then she told me to go with the secretary. I had no idea what was going on, but I felt sick with anxiety and knew something just wasn't right. My dad met me in the office and told me he was taking me home. He knelt down and looked straight at me. His eyes were brimming with a sadness I had never seen in them before, and he gave me the news: "Your...your grandfather passed away this morning. He had a heart attack and just didn't make it, Andy. Come on, get your things together and we'll go home."

I didn't cry. For a minute or two, I didn't even move. Not a muscle in my body felt alive. Not a single tear ran down my cheek. I couldn't believe what Dad had just told me. Part of me desperately prayed that it was just a nightmare, but deep down inside of me, I knew it was real. It hurt so much, as if a giant anchor was ripping my heart out, but the tears wouldn't come. Instead, I was in shock. I stood with my mouth open, and then finally moved to get my things. In a daze of grief, I somehow got my school bag and walked with Dad out to the car. I still couldn't talk. I had been rendered silent by black clouds of sadness.

The next week was by far the most difficult week of my life. It was the first time I'd ever gone to a wake and the first time I had seen a dead person resting. It was not as hard as I thought it would be, because Grampy almost looked alive. I took a long time when it was my turn to kneel by his casket and talk to him. First, I told him how much I loved him, and then I just knelt there remembering the times we'd had together. I also told him about the many questions I still had, and how I wished he could still teach me the answers. The whole time, I was looking at him, almost waiting for him to wake up. I was still hoping it was either a nightmare or a joke that would soon be over. I prayed that everything would just go back to the way it had been. Of course, that didn't happen. My Grampy was gone. This was the last time I would ever see him.

Before the funeral the next day, I made one small request. I asked if I could pick something special to have buried with him. I knew he was dead; I knew he wouldn't be using anything that was buried with him; but a small part of me believed it would make him feel better. Also, a *large* part of me knew it would make *me* feel better. Everyone seemed to agree it would be fine. The challenge was picking something that was just right. I thought about the places and the things that were important to him. So many ideas crossed my mind: his favorite wine glass, something from his garden, his flag, his sewing kit, his cooking tools, and even the bucket he'd collected mussels in. Nothing was quite right. Nothing seemed to fit in perfectly. Then I found it. It was such a simple thing, but it said so much. It was a picture my dad had taken of me on the beach, holding a striped bass I'd caught the summer after I got home. Grampy wasn't with me when I caught the fish, but that was part of why I chose it. I reached into the casket with that picture, placed it in his hand, and said, "Thank you, Grampy. Thank you for teaching me how to fish."

I still hadn't cried at all, and I was starting to become angry at myself over that. What did it mean that I couldn't cry? I was afraid people would think I wasn't really sad, or that they'd say I didn't care enough. I told myself that anyone who was sad should be crying. I thought maybe I would cry at the church, during the ceremony, but I didn't. I was chosen to be a pallbearer, helping walk my grandfather's coffin down the aisle of the church. As I held on to his coffin, draped in the American flag, I was sure I would start to cry, but I was wrong. No tears.

When we reached the graveyard, the flag on his coffin was removed and carefully folded. I was stunned when it was placed in my hands. My whole family told me he would have wanted me to have it. I felt incredibly honored, but again, as I took that flag, I was filled with wrenching sadness. I still had no tears in my eyes. More than anything, I was a completely shattered child who missed his Grampy, but I was terrified that people wouldn't see that, because I couldn't cry.

It wasn't until the funeral actually ended at the cemetery that I finally, and suddenly, began to cry. I guess I didn't cry because of the shock of his death and maybe because I could still see Grampy at the wake and funeral mass. He had died, but he was still right in front of me. Now I had to leave him. This was it. This was final. I paced all around his grave, forcing myself to think of other things to say to him. I looked at the flowers around the grave and moved them into different places. I searched for anything, any reason to stay with him as long as I could. Eventually, just like the day I went to see my mother, I had to leave, and that was when the floodgates opened and the tears came tumbling down. It was the finality of that moment that was most painful—admitting that I had to let go and walk away.

There was a reception for our family after the funeral, and I rode with my dad in the car. He did everything he could, from telling jokes to giving me hugs and back rubs, to console me and dry some of the tears. He told me how much Grampy knew I loved him and how proud he was of me. He told me some of the things Grampy had said about me and how pleased he would be that I was given the flag from his funeral. Then, my dad asked me about the picture I'd put into the casket. He had overheard my parting words. "You're really glad he taught you how to fish, huh?"

I let out a little smile and then looked up at him. I thought back to my lessons with Grampy and said, "Well, Dad, if you give a man a fish, he can eat for a day. But if you teach a man to fish, he can eat for a lifetime." He smiled back, but I don't think he understood. Something told me that he'd missed my point…it wasn't about fishing at all.

If you ask me, the most challenging puzzles in the world are often the people who live around us. I went to Truro that summer with three puzzles: my mother, my grandfather, and myself. I did not have a single clue as to how to solve them; I didn't even know where to begin. As I began to solve the puzzle of my grandfather, however, it helped me figure out the other two. In a way, my grandfather was my guide, my captain. He helped me learn about this big puzzle we call life. Simply put, Grampy taught me how to find the pieces, put them together, and then go looking for more. I love him, I miss him, and there is no way I will ever forget him.

Afterword:

The Real Life "Grampy"

This story, at least part of it, is based on real life. Part of it is based on *my* life, but most parts are fiction. I did grow up in the town of Marshfield, Massachusetts, but I was not very much like Andy at all. I certainly had my share of trouble in school, mainly because I couldn't keep my mouth shut, but the trouble was never too serious and never involved any fights. Both of my parents are still alive and well, and I also have a brother. The part that is based on real life is the character of "Grampy." When I talk about my grandfather today, I still call him by this name, and he played a very important role in my life, just as Andy's "Grampy" did.

Some of my earliest memories are of days spent with my grandparents in Hyde Park, Massachusetts. Grampy had a gift. He had a way of always making me happy. Sometimes it was a fresh bag of popcorn, other days it was a series of hilarious jokes, and some days it was a trip on his boat to go fishing in Boston Harbor. Whatever I needed, whatever I wanted, Grampy found a way to give it to me.

As I worked on <u>The Sea Shack,</u> I did not even tell him I was writing a book in his honor. I wanted it to be a surprise. If I had told him about my plan, he might have told me I was crazy. He would have been very excited and very supportive of me writing a book, but he would have named a thousand other people to honor in the book before I chose him. You see, great people never *want* to be honored, or thanked by a crowd, or showered with awards. Truly great people do great things because that is who they are; they don't see it as something extraordinary. When I finally presented him with the first published copy and explained what I had done, he did not surprise me. He told me I should not have dedicated the book to him. Although I could see the true, warm emotion in his eyes, he told me did not deserve such a tribute. It was the exact reaction I had expected, and further proof in my eyes that he truly *was* deserving of this gift.

This man, Wilbur Fisher, was amazing in so many ways. He did not have a wall covered with college degrees, but he always had a passion for reading and I don't think I have ever met a more educated man in my life. He lived a fairly quiet and reserved life, yet he earned the respect and appreciation of everyone who crossed his path. He was a man who did anything and everything for his family, from working long hours during difficult times, to buying his grandson his first bicycle. He told some of the funniest, scariest, and most interesting stories I have ever heard. He never failed to give me support and encouragement whenever I needed it. In short, he was a remarkable man to know and love, and I could not have had a better role model to admire.

Just like the character in the story, my grandfather was a veteran of World War II. He never talked too much about his time in the war, but he didn't need to. I didn't need stories to know what a great thing he did for our country. I can barely begin to imagine how horrible the fighting conditions were, but he went and did his duty with pride. I never once heard him complain about the time he spent in war and he always taught me what it meant to be a proud American. He defended the liberty and freedom I was able to grow up with, and he continued to honor and love his country every day of his life after coming home. If you ask me, that truly makes him a hero. I don't call many people heroes. I think it is a term that gets used way too often, but when I look at what my Grampy did for our country, for his family, and for me, somehow calling him a hero doesn't even seem to do him justice. His greatness, in my eyes, far exceeds even that title.

As a child, Grampy was just that—Grampy. He was another person in my family and I didn't give much thought to all the things he did. Now that I am an adult, I can truly understand the things he did. Now I can see him as a hero who bravely served his country during a long, difficult war. Now I am able to see how hard he worked after the war, just to make sure his wife and children were taken care of. Now I am able to understand what a loving grandfather he was to me, a man who was happy to spend whatever time or money he had to see me smile. I grew up with an incredible family surrounding me, and I could have written a book in tribute to many of them, but I chose my grandfather. If you asked the others in my family, I think they would all choose him, too. In so many ways, he was always a great rock for all of us to stand on. He was a shining example of so many things over my life: pride, strength, loyalty, love, commitment, respect, responsibility, and so on. He did so much for his country and all the people around him without ever looking for a reward or praise. This book was my way of thanking him for a job well done.

When the first version of <u>The Sea Shack</u> was printed, my grandfather was still alive and doing well. Unfortunately, he was diagnosed with cancer in 2005 and passed away soon afterwards. It was hard to believe a man who had been the very image of strength could be defeated by cancer so quickly and so suddenly. Before he left us, however, he had the chance to read <u>The Sea Shack</u> and enjoy it for nearly a year. I'll never forget visiting him in the hospital and hearing him tell his doctors about this book. Clearly, the tribute meant a lot to him, and seeing him describe it with such pride meant a lot to me. He was the best "Grampy" a kid could ever wish for and I am so thankful I got to honor him in a special way before his passing.

My final note of advice to you, the reader of this book, is to think about the people who have been important in *your* life and find a special way to thank them. Let them know exactly how meaningful they are and how much you care for them. I wrote this book as a gift to my grandfather, but now I realize sharing it with him was a gift to both of us. I will always cherish that time when we got to enjoy <u>The Sea Shack</u> together. For me, that year became the perfect final chapter to a truly wonderful story.

About the Author:

Mark McNulty has dedicated his career to working with children of all ages. He has worked as an elementary school teacher in two states and made multiple author visits to schools and reading groups. He has also organized creative writing workshops in grades two through eight. He continues to work on his writing from his home in Massachusetts, creating new stories that will be enjoyed by children and adults alike.

His writing and his teaching are both supported by his own education. He holds two Bachelor's degrees from Boston College: one in elementary education and moderate special needs, the other in communications. He also holds a Master's degree in education from Fitchburg State College. He continues to enroll in graduate level courses and attend various writing workshops and conferences to expand his own learning.

When he is not writing or working, Mark enjoys many interests and hobbies. These include fishing, snorkeling, skiing, boating, and vacationing on New Hampshire's Lake Winnipesaukee. Mark also likes to travel whenever he has the opportunity. Among his favorite destinations are the Caribbean Islands, Florida's Gulf Coast, San Diego, and Galway, Ireland. Finally, he is an avid sports fan. The Boston Red Sox, Bruins, Patriots, and Celtics are all very close to his heart, along with his Boston College Eagles.

Mark McNulty welcomes feedback from all readers. Feel free to contact him at any time or visit his blog:

E-Mail: mcnulty1977@gmail.com

Twitter: @mcnulty1977

facebook: Mark McNulty – Writer

**Blog address:
http://mark-mcnulty.blogspot.com**

25547430R00162

Made in the USA
Lexington, KY
27 August 2013